LOVE IN LAVENDER LANE

Fiona exchanges her quiet suburban world for 1970s London when she inherits her great-aunt's marriage bureau near Marble Arch. But she has never been truly in love, so it's going to be a challenge arranging perfect pairings for her starry-eyed clients . . . While Fiona's busy interviewing and arranging introductions, how will she ever find time to make her own dream come true? And could it be that she and her most difficult client to match are actually meant for one another?

JILL BARRY

LOVE IN LAVENDER LANE

Complete and Unabridged

LINFORD
Leicester

First published in Great Britain in 2020

First Linford Edition
published 2021

*A catalogue record for this book is available
from the British Library.*

ISBN 978–1–4448–4733–8

Published by
Ulverscroft Limited
Anstey, Leicestershire

Printed and bound in Great Britain by
TJ Books Ltd., Padstow, Cornwall

This book is printed on acid-free paper

Changes on the Horizon

Fiona reached her gate then jumped as her mother called from the front door.

'I'm sorry, love. I didn't mean to alarm you.'

Fiona shut the gate and hurried up the path.

'What's the matter, Mum?' Her mother drew her inside and hugged her.

'Oh, Fi! I just got a phone call saying your great-aunt Millie has passed away. Your dad's watching 'Charlie's Angels' so I thought I'd tell him after it finished.'

Fiona took her hands.

'I'm so sorry. Who gave you the news?'

'Aunt Millie's secretary. Apparently, Millie complained of feeling unwell when the young woman let herself in yesterday morning. She was having difficulty in breathing so Katie, I think her name is, dialled 999 at once, but sadly your great-aunt became unconscious and it was all over by this afternoon.'

'Thank goodness Katie was around,

even though there was a sad ending.' Fiona bit her lip. 'I wish we could have seen more of Great-aunt Millie, but I know you used to visit her when you and Dad lived near London.'

Mrs Maple led the way to the kitchen. Fiona reached down a cup and saucer and joined her mother at the table.

'She was always very kind to us,' Mrs Maple said. 'We didn't have much money to spare back then so sometimes she'd treat us to the theatre.

'It was tragic Millie was widowed so young, but she was born in that generation World War II hit hard.'

'Didn't she become a school matron somewhere up north?'

'Yes, after she was widowed, she took that job and remained at the school for years. When she inherited the property where her parents had lived, she moved back to London.

'A few years later, your dad and I moved away because of his job and I asked her a couple of times to come and stay with us, but she always insisted she hated travelling. I feel guilty now that I didn't make more effort to visit her.'

'I went once or twice with you. She took us to tea in Harrods, didn't she? I remember telling my friends about it, I was so thrilled.'

'Do you remember where she lived?'

'Of course. It was down a little alley, not far from Marble Arch. And she ran some kind of office, didn't she? I remember asking her what she did, but she waved her hand in the air and said something about slotting people into the right places.'

'Yes, I believe it was some kind of employment agency, but she was a private kind of person so I didn't press the matter.'

'I remember seeing a door marked 'Office' when we went to see her, but she took us straight upstairs and her flat was spilling over with furniture showing what good taste she had.'

'I wonder what will happen to all of it now.' Fiona's mum drained her cup. 'I'm not aware of any relations besides your dad and us.'

'I hope she enjoyed whatever it was she was doing. It must be wonderful to find something that makes you pleased to go on working at it.'

'Hmm.' Fiona's mum was biting the edge of her forefinger — always a sign that something was niggling at her.

★ ★ ★

Two days later, Fiona Maple left the house in a hurry. She'd been feeling discontented with her office job for a while and when she did sleep, her dreams were full of people she didn't know. She slept through her alarm until her mother called to her.

Fiona hated being late for work and it didn't help her mood to find a ladder in her tights when she reached the office cloakroom.

Unusually, her boss, Mr Clark, was in a tetchy mood because he'd mislaid a file. Fortunately, he calmed down after his secretary located it but Fiona found herself clock-watching and wondering again whether she should start looking for another job. Maybe what she needed was a complete change of lifestyle.

She walked home as usual but got caught in a rain shower and as she'd rushed out that morning and chosen a jacket with no hood, she let herself into number 111 Elm Tree Gardens feeling wet and miserable.

'I'm home, Mum,' Fiona called as she removed her soggy jacket and hung it up to dry. As she wriggled her feet out of her high-heeled shoes, her mother appeared in the kitchen doorway, holding an official-looking brown envelope.

'Goodness, Fi, you look like a drowned rat!'

'It's horrible out there, Mum. I need to go straight upstairs and dry my hair.'

'Well, get yourself sorted out while I finish the supper. This letter came for you today, but it can wait. I wondered if you'd made a job application, since you've been so restless lately.'

'Funnily enough, I have been wondering about having a change but I haven't done anything about it yet. I've no idea what that letter's about but I'll be as quick as I can.'

* * *

'Spring's taking its time to get going.' Mrs Maple glanced at the rain beating a tattoo on the kitchen window.

'Yes, those are more than just April showers. Something smells good.'

'Your father said he'll be late back so I made a chicken casserole. I can leave his on low in the oven.'

'Uhuh.' Fiona was peering at her letter. The postmark was a blur but her name and address typed neatly on the envelope showed this letter was official. She nudged her fingernail at the side of the gummed flap and gently prised open the envelope. Inside was a thick sheet of cream notepaper, which when she unfolded it and read the embossed dark blue heading, made her gasp.

'What on earth! I haven't a clue what this is all about.' Swiftly she scanned the page. Was she imagining things? Fiona shook her head. She closed her eyes and opened them again. 'You'll never guess what this says!'

'It's not a speeding offence, is it?' Her mother was frowning.

'Of course not, Mum. '

'You don't have to tell me if you don't want to.'

'Mmm?' Fiona glanced up. 'Let me read it to you. It's dated May 2nd, 1975, and it says, 'Dear Miss Maple, I'm sorry I had to ring your mother with the sad news of my employer's passing. Mrs Maple was always kind to me and it was a pleasure to work for her for the last seven years.

'Your great-aunt left detailed instructions as to what to do should anything happen to her. You will be hearing from her solicitors, of course, but she wanted me to contact you first, to advise you she has bequeathed her property to you in her last will and testament.

'But there is one important condition attached. And that is for you to take over the running of Mrs Maple's Marriage Bureau. Should you decide not to accept this requirement, the property would be sold and the money given to your great-aunt's favourite charity.

'I'm aware that you haven't visited Lavender Lane for a while, but I want you to know the property is in good repair and you'll be able to move into the apartment above the offices as soon as possible. This is a specific request made by your great-aunt and included in her will.

'Mrs Maple knew this bequest would come as a shock to you and she hoped you would see fit to retain my services as your secretary.

'I understand this may not meet with your approval but meantime I can assure you, I shall do my best to keep the office running smoothly for as long as necessary. Needless to say, I very much hope you can take up your new role as soon as possible. Yours sincerely, Katie Armstrong (Secretary).'

Fiona handed the letter to her mother

who stared at the letter heading in disbelief.

'My goodness, I had no idea what Millie was involved in.'

'I'm stunned,' Fiona said. 'I never dreamed Great-aunt Millie would include me in her will, especially as she hardly knew me.'

'Maybe not,' her mum said thoughtfully, 'but when we did speak on the phone, she'd always ask how you were doing. A while back, I happened to mention you weren't too thrilled with your job and she asked whether you'd ever thought of working in London.

'I would've mentioned it to you but you'd just begun seeing Daniel so I kept quiet.' Mrs Maple bit her lip.

'Don't look so worried, Mum. Since Daniel and I stopped seeing one another, I've thought about spreading my wings but maybe you look after me too well.'

'So, what do you think?'

'About taking over the business?'

'Yes. The Marriage Bureau, no less.' Mrs Maple gave a wry smile. 'Millie kept that under her hat all right! Who'd have thought it? You'll become a property owner now — something that doesn't happen to many single women, now does it? I wonder what your dad will say.'

Fiona stared at her mother, the significance of this windfall only now beginning to sink in.

'I'm still reeling from the news. I've never even rented a flat on my own, let alone one in London. Anyway, how on earth could I run a business I know absolutely nothing about?

'Was Great-aunt Millie actually advising people who they should marry?'

'Don't ask me, love! I know these places exist but your dad and I met at a church social, thank goodness.'

'I don't know what it's like to fall in love.' Fiona couldn't help blushing. 'So how could I possibly become a matchmaker? The whole thing's out of the question, even though I'd become a property owner. I have to say no, don't I?'

In at the Deep End

But next day, Fiona felt differently. Her boss proved surprisingly helpful after she handed in her notice. Mr Clark listened while she told him about her unexpected bequest, raising his eyebrows when he learned the terms of the will.

She decided not to mention the nature of her aunt's business, and used the employment bureau tag her mother had mentioned, telling herself it wasn't so much an untruth as a way of preventing embarrassment.

After all, some people still regarded finding a partner with such an organisation as a stigma.

'This will be a big challenge for you,' her boss said. 'But no-one can blame you for seizing the opportunity. You've been a good secretary, Fiona. But you must start your new life as soon as possible. I'll make sure your wages are paid up to date and of course you must take your remaining days of leave instead of working out your notice.'

'Shall I ring the temping agency?' she asked.

'That would be most helpful.' He gave her a rare smile. 'We'll all miss you, you know.'

He'd chatted a little to her about London, wished her well and told her if things didn't work out, he was happy to give her a first-class reference.

She couldn't help feeling her great-aunt had expected too much of her, but now things were in motion and when she wasn't quaking with fear, she was thanking her lucky stars for giving her such an exciting opportunity.

Later, walking home, Fiona decided that if she hated living in London and carrying out what still seemed to her an impossible task, there could be no going back. She would take each day as it came.

And she'd set off on her own, even though she risked her mum feeling affronted at not being asked to hold her hand. She felt it was important to stand on her own two feet right from the start.

She'd arranged with Katie Armstrong that she'd take the train to London on Saturday morning and that Katie would be at the office ready to let her in.

Mr Maple insisted on giving his daughter money for a taxi from Paddington to Marble Arch and wouldn't take no for an answer. Now, sitting in the back of the big black Hackney cab, her suitcase beside her, she was grateful for her dad's thoughtfulness, especially as she was pretty clueless as to how to find her way around the city.

She kept wondering what Katie Armstrong was like. The letter she'd sent was written quite formally and in the one brief telephone conversation they'd had, Millie's secretary had confirmed in a very well-articulated manner, how she'd written down Fiona's arrival time and would be waiting for her.

★ ★ ★

Paddington Station was as cavernous, dirty and noisy as Fiona remembered

13

it. People of all nationalities, ages and sizes milled around, checking train times and hurrying towards various departure points.

She lugged her suitcase along the platform and through the barrier, following the signs to the taxi drop off and pick up area.

She'd heard about cab drivers who liked putting the world to rights and hers lived up to the image. To her relief, he stopped talking about whether or not the UK should be in the European Community or not and asked how long she'd be staying and whether she was starting a new job or holidaying with relations as she wasn't heading for a hotel.

She said her friend would be waiting for her and questioned him about some of the landmarks they were passing.

'Marble Arch comin' up on yer left,' he said as he stopped at the traffic lights. 'Very handy if you fancy a stroll in the park.' He turned down the next road on the right and continued towards the end of it.

'Here you go, darling,' he said, pulling into the kerbside. 'That's Lavender Lane, just down there.'

He hoisted her suitcase from the cab while Fiona got her money ready.

'Mind how yer go,' he said, giving her a wave as he clambered back behind the steering wheel.

Standing alone on the pavement, looking down the mews she vaguely remembered from that last visit with her mum, Fiona took a deep breath and set off down the alley, checking the numbers as she went.

Outside the door of number 7 Lavender Lane stood a small tub containing a lavender plant, though it was as yet too early for it to bloom. Somehow it seemed like a hopeful sign, though she had no idea why.

Fiona pushed the doorbell and stood waiting. Within moments she heard footsteps, then silence before the door opened a few inches and she saw the safety chain in place. Sensible.

'Miss Armstrong? I'm Fiona Maple.'

The door swung wide and a tall, dark-haired young woman was smiling a welcome.

'Yes, you're in the right place, Miss Maple. I saw the cab pull up outside. Your train must have been on time, then?'

'Yes, thanks. Goodness, you look much younger than I expected!'

Katie Armstrong chuckled.

'I'm not that young, you know. Let me take your case.' She lifted the big brown suitcase inside and Fiona followed in its wake.

'I'm afraid there's a flight of stairs up to the flat, but I'll lock up again, then show you round. I've filled the kettle ready and I bought a few cakes in case you're peckish. The flat's lovely — but then you probably remember it from visiting before?'

'You're very kind. To be honest, Miss Armstrong, I'm still trying to figure out whether all this is actually happening to me.'

'I should have told you I'm married but please call me Katie.' She turned

16

away from the door.

'I shall, and you must call me Fiona.' She held out her hand to the other girl. 'Pleased to meet you. Now, follow me and we'll soon have you feeling at home.'

Fiona doubted that, but now she was really here and not just imagining how things would be, the thought of living in her own apartment, with no-one to please but herself, was too exciting for words.

Yet, as she followed Katie up the stairs, she began to feel like the country mouse she believed she was.

Her demure little two-piece suit in a misty shade of blue wool, always made her feel smart when she wore it but Katie's outfit was far more stylish than anything Fiona owned. And it seemed much warmer here in the city than it had at home.

She eyed Katie's black platform-heel shoes, rust-coloured flared trousers and emerald green short-sleeved jumper and felt a flash of envy, likening herself to Miss Moneypenny against Katie's Bond girl image.

'Here we are.' Katie parked the case and waited for Fiona to join her.

They'd reached a small landing with one door ajar.

'You go first,' Katie said. 'I left the door half-open on purpose. Welcome to your new home.'

Fiona smiled at her, actually afraid to speak in case a sob popped out instead.

But she knew she mustn't think of the past, mustn't feel guilty at not having kept in touch with her great-aunt and definitely mustn't feel ashamed for not looking like a London dolly-bird. She pushed the door open and stepped inside.

Fiona found herself in a small hallway, carpeted in ruby red. Her gaze took in five doors, each one painted jet black with its panels highlighted in gold.

Katie cleared her throat.

'The décor's a bit dated, but Mrs Maple loved it. There's no reason why you can't have something different.'

'I don't dislike it.' Fiona turned to face her. 'It's just so different from home.

I must have seen it when I came here last but I seem to remember more about the sitting-room and all my great-aunt's lovely things.'

Katie smiled.

'All yours now,' she said. 'Are you happy if I make our tea up here? There's a kettle in my little office downstairs if you prefer.' She hesitated.

'I don't want you to feel I'm trying to take you over. This apartment is your personal and private space and normally I wouldn't be up here.'

'Gosh, I should be making tea for you, really! But please go ahead. And you must let me pay you back for the cakes you bought.'

'My treat. I'll be through that door when you're ready.'

Left alone, Fiona thought back to her last visit and pushed open the nearest door. As she anticipated, it was the bathroom, complete with avocado suite. Everything looked in good order and the taps on the washbasin and the clawfoot bath positively gleamed.

The only bedroom was the next door along and she didn't recall being shown it before. The double bed with its wooden headboard, beautifully carved with rosebuds and ferns, couldn't have been more different from her own pink velveteen-covered one at home.

But though the wardrobe and dressing table before the window were solid and obviously long-standing, the room had an airy feel. The dark-green shutters were pulled apart and the window was half open, allowing a gentle breeze to play with the pastel green curtains.

Fiona walked over and peered out. On her arrival, she'd been so intent on paying the taxi driver and gathering her belongings, she had hardly noticed her surroundings. Trees were showing off their early summer finery against the sombre brick-terraced houses, and the Victorian lamp-posts, with their elegant lanterns, reminded her of a Dickensian TV drama series.

She could almost imagine Bob Cratchit, not yet prepared to put away his long, woollen muffler, hurrying along the pavements, ready to toil another long day at the beck and call of his miserly boss.

Fiona, having wondered how she'd cope with moving into her aunt's domain so soon after her departure, felt surprisingly content. Katie must have made up the bed with crisp white linen of a quality Fiona wasn't used to.

Of course, it was sad to think of such a lively old lady living alone for so many years, but that had been how she preferred it.

The family had been taken aback to learn Millie had put her foot down regarding her funeral. No-one was to attend besides the necessary professionals. Her aunt had been a free spirit and how Fiona wished she knew more about her. Her eye was caught by a picture on the dressing table and she hurried across to inspect it.

The young woman's oval countenance and dark hair, drawn back from her face, was dominated by a pair of dark, long-lashed eyes. She wore a short-sleeved dress with a pretty round collar. But the wow factor was the love and joy shining from her eyes and taking Fiona's breath away.

Tears welled up as she gazed at the twenty-year-old Millie and her fiancé, Robert Maple, who had been her father's Uncle Bob.

He wore his RAF uniform, looking both handsome and proud beside his pretty fiancée. They'd married before Bob rejoined his squadron in Cambridgeshire to commence training on the big Lancaster Bomber aircraft.

Fiona needed to scrabble in her pocket for a handkerchief as she imagined her aunt across the years, whispering a 'Goodnight sweetheart' to her husband before settling down to sleep. How sad that Great-aunt Millie hadn't had the joy of bringing up a family with her husband.

Fiona gulped, blew her nose and made a decision. Each night from now on, when she got into bed, she'd whisper a loving goodnight to the couple. Maybe they were together again now? As soon as she thought that, it was as though she could hear Great-aunt Millie telling her to get on with her new life. Wasn't that what she was here for?

She'd peep at the sitting-room then join Katie. She wanted to prove Millie had shown good judgement in leaving everything to her great-niece and already she'd made her first important decision.

'Tea's brewing,' Katie called as Fiona entered the kitchen.

'I've only just realised I'm parched. Breakfast seems ages ago.'

'That's because it probably was.' As Katie put a plate of cakes on the table in the window, Fiona glanced at the slender gold band on her ring finger but was afraid to ask about her husband, in case there was a story here that might also be a sad one, although Katie had said she was married.

'Sit down and I'll bring our tea over,' Katie said.

'I feel guilty about you waiting on me.'

'Please don't. It's your first day in the

capital.' Katie carried the tray over to Fiona. 'Milk in first? I'll let you pour the tea if that makes you feel better.'

'I think I can manage that.' Fiona was getting to like her new companion. Maybe this was the moment to confide her decision? Though becoming used to wearing Millie's shoes would take some doing.

'I guess it was you who moved all Great-aunt Millie's clothing from the bedroom?'

'I hope I did right.' Katie looked a tad worried.

'Of course you did and it was kind of you to put everything in the box-room. What do you suggest we do with it all?

'Again, Mrs Maple had a plan, bless her. I'll need to contact someone I know who deals in second-hand garments, but you might like to sort through the jewellery.'

'Perhaps we could do that together some time? I'd like you to select something as a keepsake.'

Katie smiled.

'That's a lovely idea. But there is a little gift of cash coming my way, I believe.'

'Good. I'd still like you to choose something, though at the moment I can't help thinking how tempting those cakes look!' Fiona eyed the fruit tartlets, thinking they were far superior to the offerings at her hometown bakery. But these were probably twice the price!

Her dad had talked about London's high cost of living and Fiona knew she'd need to ask Katie's advice about where best to shop.

'Dig in,' Katie said. 'I thought we'd have a treat today. These came from a French patisserie not far from here but I try not to go there too often. It's Temptation Alley!'

Fiona placed a fruit tart on her plate. Luscious black cherries nestled on a cushion of creamy custard inside a fluted pastry case.

'Before I eat anything, I need to ask you something, Katie.'

'Ask away.' Katie placed both hands in her lap and sat still, her eyes on Fiona.

'You mentioned my great-aunt's wish that you should remain in your position as secretary?'

'That's right.'

Fiona, seeing Katie's expression change, hurried to explain herself.

'There are two sides to this, you know. I've made up my mind I'd be crazy to let you go.' She held up her hand.

'Before you say anything, I want you to know I've had several years of experience as a secretary, but as for the core business — the, um, clients of the bureau, I feel I'm heading into the unknown.

'Without you to guide me, I don't think I have any hope of making Millie's wish come true so yes, I want you to stay on, Katie. But you also have a say in this. Do you think you'd be happy working with me?'

Katie looked down at her hands. Fiona hardly dared breathe. What would the answer be?

Katie took a handkerchief from her pocket and pressed it to her lips.

'Katie? Are you OK?'

As if the sun had suddenly come out, Katie's smile lit up the room. 'Never been better! I just felt a bit emotional, that's all. Goodness me, Fiona, you remind me so much of Millie.

'She was white-haired when I first knew her but I've seen photographs of her when she was young and it's obvious you've inherited her beautiful tresses. Yes, please, I'd be honoured to stay on as your secretary.'

'That's such a relief. But from now on, I want you to describe yourself as my personal assistant. I'm sure you're carrying out that role at the moment. But if you're signing a letter on my behalf or introducing yourself to a new client, please state your new title.'

'Thank you very much. Except, regarding new clients, the problem is, they're like snowdrops in August at the moment.'

'Really?'

'I'm afraid so. We had only one new inquiry this week and he's coming to see us on Tuesday.'

'Would I be able to sit in while you

talk to him?'

'I'm so sorry, Fiona. Some weeks ago, I asked Mrs Maple if I could book myself a day's holiday for this coming Tuesday. It's my grandmother's seventieth birthday lunch in Brighton and I'll be travelling down on Monday evening. I'm afraid you'll need to interview Captain Carlisle on your own.'

Asking the Right Questions

After tea, Fiona accompanied her new personal assistant to the bus stop. Katie had rummaged in the cupboard under the stairs for a shopping bag.

'On the way, I'll show you a corner shop where you can buy groceries,' she said. 'You'll find milk and butter in the fridge and there's a small white loaf in the breadbin and a pot of my mother's homemade marmalade in the cupboard.'

'That's very thoughtful of you. On Monday we must discuss your salary and talk about a petty cash allowance. When you're not teaching me how to deal with clients!'

'I think you'll be fine. Mrs Maple used to say, let them do most of the talking. Make notes and don't forget to ask permission to take their picture, though some prefer to bring their own photo.'

'You make it sound easy,' Fiona said glumly.

'People are fascinating. You're going

to learn a lot about human nature, you mark my words.' Katie stopped at the junction of two roads. 'The shop's just down there. Mr Kumar is very helpful and he adored your great-aunt so be sure to mention who you are. Millie had an account, which I've settled out of the petty cash, but you can choose how you run things, of course.

'And if you need help with anything, you'll find my home phone number beside the office phone. I'd better run now, but don't worry about a thing and I'll see you on Monday morning.'

A quick wave and she was on her way. Fiona stood, watching the trim figure disappear round the next corner. She really was on her own now.

But inside the shop, she found it well-stocked and purchased enough provisions to last her a few days.

She also heard quite a lot of Mr Kumar's life story but was saved when his wife appeared and told him it was time for his tea break. Both he and Mrs Kumar said they were sad to hear about

Mrs Maple but wished Fiona well in her new life. She left the shop, feeling pleased with the Londoners she'd met over the last few hours.

Letting herself in to number 7 Lavender Lane, Fiona coped with the door locks, stowed her purchases and decided she was too tired for a walk so might as well inspect the office before making her evening meal.

Earlier, Katie had thought it best not to overwhelm the new arrival with the business side of things and now Fiona was feeling grateful about the decision. No harm in taking a look, though.

She unlocked the room where presumably clients waited until entering Mrs Maple's domain. Both the inner doors were locked but Fiona began with Katie's office which was small, tidy and well decorated. Both offices contained filing cabinets so needed yet more keys from the bunch, making Fiona feel like an old-fashioned housekeeper or matron.

The big diary on what would be her own desk was already open at the new week. She sat down to read what she now recognised as Katie's handwriting, her gaze fixing on Tuesday's 11 o'clock appointment with Captain Timothy Carlisle.

Beside it was an index card on which was written the new client's date of birth, home address and telephone number.

What story, Fiona mused, would be revealed about the airline pilot's decision to consult a marriage bureau? Surely someone in his position must be surrounded by beautiful girls?

She had only flown on one occasion but she remembered seeing some of the flight crews walking through the terminal building, both the men and the women looking well-groomed and attractive.

Captains wore four gold hoops round their sleeves, distinguishing them from their juniors. She hoped her new client wouldn't be too arrogant or pernickety.

Suddenly she felt very tired. But she must ring her parents because they'd be sure to worry if they didn't hear from her soon. Fiona picked up the receiver and made the first telephone call of her new life.

★ ★ ★

Fiona spent Sunday quietly. She walked in Hyde Park, enjoying the fresh air and watching the people strolling rather than hurrying along.

She bought a newspaper on her way back to Lavender Lane, determined to discover what kind of advertisements her opposition used. Katie's pronouncement about new clients being thin on the ground was worrying her and she needed to investigate it.

She spent the afternoon checking clients' files so she was a little better informed for the next day, and after she locked up and returned to the apartment, she was ready to sit down with the Sunday papers.

Fingers trembling, she riffled through the pages of her father's favourite newspaper until she reached the personal columns. Some of the insertions puzzled

33

her but she shook her head and concentrated on finding the ones she was after.

Mary Silver's Introduction Agency was seeking single young ladies under the age of thirty-five to meet discerning gentlemen up to the age of forty-five. Fiona pursed her lips. What about the unfortunate ladies who were above that age barrier?

Below this advertisement, a firm called Superior Singles invited ladies and gentlemen who sought companionship to contact their box number. For a moment, Fiona considered enquiring under a false name then scolded herself for even thinking of such a thing. She would be furious if someone wasted her time in such a way.

The Palmer Street Agency was aiming at lonely country gentlemen and women who despaired of ever meeting someone to spend the rest of their life with. Fiona wondered how well it would work if someone living in Perth seemed ideally suited to a person from Paddington.

Dropping the paper on the floor, she

rose and wandered across to the window. A moment of panic hit her as she asked herself how she could possibly guide lonely men and women to the altar?

She had never known what it was like to fall in love, whereas her great-aunt had been head-over-heels with her young husband.

Millie must have floated on a fluffy pink cloud of happiness until she'd been widowed and decided to spend her later years helping others find the same contentment.

If Millie knew how lacking in confidence her great-niece was about playing matchmaker, she'd probably throw up her hands in despair and tell her to get on with it! Those women who had lived through the War knew a thing or two about survival.

Fiona lacked Millie's experience, yet she'd been entrusted with her business. And never mind potential new clients — for a start, she needed to set about helping the existing ones towards wedded bliss.

It was almost as though she could hear Great-aunt Millie sighing with relief as Fiona remembered she actually possessed a backbone and a kind heart. But did she truly imagine she could work miracles?

* * *

On Monday morning Fiona was up early and preparing a list of questions she thought suitable to ask a new client. Once she started, she could hardly bear to stop and make herself tea and toast. With the radio playing in the background while she stood by the grill watching bread slices turn pale brown, she suddenly realised she was hearing Frankie Valli singing 'My Eyes Adored You'.

Could popular song titles help her come up with an imaginative advertisement?

Taking her breakfast over to the table, she decided she and Katie should have a proper meeting with an agenda which her assistant would have no problem in composing.

But Fiona knew she must prepare herself for her Tuesday morning appointment. Even though many women were carrying out important roles in all kinds of areas, many men still resisted the idea of a female being in charge of them.

But surely a man would prefer to speak to a woman when it came to affairs of the heart?

★　★　★

By five past nine, Katie and Fiona were sitting in the big office, files open before them.

'I need to clear out some of the very old ones,' Katie said. 'Now you're here and working full-time, I'll be able to do some sorting.'

'How long do we keep a client's file?' Fiona looked up.

'Mrs Maple liked to hang on to the papers for at least eight years. She reckoned if a couple lasted beyond the seven-year itch, their details could be destroyed.'

'What's the reason for keeping files belonging to clients who couldn't be matched?'

'Good question. Some clients have been known to return to us after opting not to stay registered any longer. Having all their details helps us re-register rather than begin from the beginning.'

'Does a leopard ever change his spots in real life?'

Katie laughed.

'Another good question! In some ways, yes, possibly. Some people 'see the light' as they say, and become regular churchgoers. Others might have taken up a sport or become a vegetarian, learned to play a musical instrument or speak another language. Things like that could influence their choice of people they'd like to meet.'

'I see.' Fiona reached for her list. 'Could I ask you to look at this? I know you'll advise me how to conduct an interview but I wondered if I was on the right track.

'I looked at some of the client information yesterday but also came up with a few questions of my own.' She held out the list.

'Well done.' Katie began reading. 'Yes, knowing the client's date of birth is vital. Some people are adamant about a prospective partner's age. And don't let them get away with telling you it's August 1945. I've interviewed several women with a firm belief in the star signs and wanting to know whether John Smith was Mr Leo or Mr Libra.'

'Or Lord Libra?'

'Oh, yes, we have our share of titled clients.' Katie looked back at Fiona's list.

'Religion, yes. Occupation also. Marital status, too. It's not enough just to know someone's a single lady or gentleman. They might be widowed or divorced, remember.'

'And might then have dependent children?'

'That's it. Whether they have dependent adult relatives is also useful to know. We once had someone who said she could only marry a man who didn't mind her bringing her elderly mother to live with them.'

'Goodness.' Fiona blinked hard. 'I can understand how most men could be put off by that condition.'

'I see your next one is to ask if they're solvent.'

Fiona made a face.

'Yes — it seems very intrusive to question them about money but I thought I'd better include it.'

'You're right. We don't expect to know anyone's exact income but people understandably might be put off to know a prospective partner was deep in debt.' She was nodding now.

'I see you've included asking whether the person likes animals. Do they own a pet and if so, what? That's very important.'

'Though if someone wasn't used to dogs, for example, they might discover what they'd been missing!'

'A good point. But if someone's frightened of them or allergic to cats or has a phobia about caged birds, that's a very important thing to bear in mind.'

'I don't think I put smoking on the list. Would that be a problem?'

'Do you smoke, Fiona?'

Fiona shook her head.

'My parents used to but they've both given up.'

'If you had a boyfriend who smoked, would that worry you?'

Fiona sat back in her chair.

'Oh, dear. I can see how difficult it would be to become too finicky over certain things. I think it'd depend how fond I was of the chap.'

'Well, there you are. There are certain areas where people can reach a compromise and others that are too big an obstacle.'

'Ha! Yes, I definitely agree with that.'

'You sound as though you speak from the heart.' Katie paused. 'But please don't think you have to comment.'

'It's OK. I stopped seeing someone not that long ago, simply because he never thought for himself. Always asked me what I thought and what I wanted to do when we were going out.'

'It's strange, isn't it? Katie said. 'We don't want a man to be domineering or always assume he knows best, but if he's a drip, we don't like that, either!'

The pair exchanged glances and laughed.

'Was your boyfriend heartbroken when you ended things?'

'Hardly. He was more concerned over being stuck with a couple of tickets for a dance and no-one to go with.'

'So, you're not involved with anyone at the moment?'

'That's right. And I'm not likely to meet anyone here, even if I wanted to!'

'You'll be meeting men, that's for sure.'

'Yes, but only as part of my job. I shan't be mixing business with pleasure. Surely that would be a disastrous thing to do!'

Not a Great Start

The telephone interrupted and Katie picked up on the fifth ring, mouthing something Fiona decoded as 'Mustn't appear too eager!'

'Mrs Maple's Marriage Bureau. How may I help you?'

Fiona kept her pen and notepad handy in case she needed to jot down anything of importance. Even while secretly dreading her first client interview the next day, she hoped the pilot wasn't ringing to postpone or, even worse, to cancel his appointment. But she soon relaxed.

'We'd be delighted if you came to see us. I'm Mrs Maple's personal assistant, Katie Armstrong. May I take your name and contact telephone number, please?' She began to write down the information before reading it back and listening again.

'I'll just check the diary. Won't keep you a moment.'

Fiona pushed the big diary across the

table.

'Friday morning, you said? How far away are you? Oh, Greenwich, how lovely. What about eleven o'clock? Yes, we can do half-past ten if that suits you better.'

Katie wrote the details in the diary and proceeded to explain exactly how to find the offices while Fiona wondered if the person was male or female.

She'd learned that the number of current clients who were trying to find their soulmate were about even as regarded their gender.

Katie put the phone down.

'Sounds really pleasant. A young woman who's a primary school teacher. Very realistic. Says she has thick ankles and wears specs but she might suit a young man who isn't exactly romantic hero material, either!'

'She does sound lovely. How exciting! A new inquiry on my first morning in the office. Which reminds me, you won't forget to coach me ready for the dashing captain tomorrow, will you, Katie?'

'Of course not. Let me show you how we deal with a first inquiry, over the phone or in the post.

'If they make an appointment for an interview, we put their basic details on one of these cards here, then place it in the index box. They get a file as soon as they request a meeting. Now, if I might make a suggestion . . .'

'Please do, Katie. I can do with all the help I can get.'

The other girl nodded.

'I'm sure you'll soon be up and running but it might be better if you spend the next few days becoming used to the office system and carrying out the interviews for new clients — just two at the moment.'

'Well, it's certainly going to be a baptism of fire when I meet Captain Carlisle. Poor man, I hope he doesn't guess I'm quaking at the thought of putting my foot in it.'

'You've already shown how interested you are and you have the standard questions at your fingertips. I can't advise you as to how you guide the conversation.

'Once you've written down the basic information, you can always start by asking him how he'd describe himself if asked to write a short piece to place in the personal column of a newspaper.'

She sat back and waved her pen at Fiona.

'In fact, why don't we each have a go at doing that now? We should also write down what kind of qualities we'd look for when hoping to find a husband. It's what Mrs Maple asked me to do when she interviewed me, so are you game?'

★ ★ ★

Fiona was still writing when Katie completed her own list and headed to her own office to switch on the kettle. Several minutes later, Fiona laid down her pen. The page in front of her contained several crossings out but she'd managed to find three facts about herself that she considered important.

However, she'd come up with six or seven qualities which she thought were significant as good husband material. When her new assistant brought two cups of tea into the office and sat down again, Fiona decided to be bold.

'Katie, I hope you won't mind me asking this, but could I enquire about Mr Armstrong?' She offered up a quick prayer as to Katie's other half's wellbeing.

What a relief when Katie grinned.

'Ask away. And it's Dr Armstrong. He's currently on a cruise liner, working as the ship's medical officer, so I'm on my own for a couple more months.'

'Goodness, how interesting. How did you two find one another?' Fiona ignored her cup of tea. This was much more fascinating.

'We met at my cousin's wedding down in Brighton almost four years ago. Thomas, or Tommy as I call him, was there on his own, as I was, and we spotted one another but it took a while before he plucked up courage to come over and speak to me.'

'Can you remember what he said?'

'He introduced himself first and checked

I wasn't spoken for.' Katie's cheeks flushed a delicate shade of pink. 'I thought how polite he was and how his eyes were kind and a lovely shade of bluey-green.'

'Was it love at first sight?'

'Not really. I was a bit overawed by his profession. I was just a lowly shorthand typist hoping to find myself a proper secretarial job.'

Fiona nodded her head.

'That's how I started out. So, what happened next?'

'We talked about my cousin and the bridegroom whom Tommy had gone to school with. They're both ten years older than me but I didn't let that stand in my way.' She laughed.

'Looking back, maybe I did feel a little more than interest that first time we met. Tommy insists he made up his mind he wanted to marry me the moment we began chatting.'

'That's so romantic! You're a very lucky girl — and he's a lucky man, of course.'

'We think so. But come on, let's see what each of us has written, shall we?'

'You go first,' Fiona said without hesitation.

'Coward!' But Katie was laughing. 'OK. I see myself as practical, confident and home-loving but sometimes I don't see the bigger picture.

'I'd always longed to find a man who was taller than me, cleverer than me but not overbearing with it. And someone having a good sense of humour was important, too, so, my goodness, I hit the jackpot! Though Tommy would argue being a doctor's wife isn't exactly a bed of roses.'

'You'd prefer him to be at home more, obviously.'

'We're working on that. One day, he hopes to find a country practice. I'm happy with that as long as it's somewhere I can visit London from, when I want to see my parents or fancy a day out.'

Fiona made a face.

'Thanks for telling me this, but from a selfish point of view, I hope that doesn't happen too soon.'

'I doubt it will. Now, your turn, boss!'

Fiona nodded.

'You did say important qualities, not necessarily good ones, so here we go. I think I'm considerate of others and quite patient — except I did reach a point when I knew I had to break things off with my last boyfriend. Does that make me ruthless?'

'No,' Katie said. 'It would have been unkind to let the young man go on thinking everything was fine — not at all a good foundation for any relationship. And what qualities have you come up with regarding a soulmate?'

'My ideal man should be considerate, quite dominant but not domineering. Able to laugh at himself and at me as well as with me. He doesn't need to be a six-footer but I'd prefer if he didn't have blond hair or a moustache or beard. Why are you smiling?'

'Tommy's stopped shaving while he's at sea. I'm rather looking forward to seeing my bearded husband! But I think, if you met someone who set the sparks flying, you mightn't be so fussy about his hair colouring.'

'Maybe, but it's unlikely to happen. I'll be too busy helping our clients find their ideal match, won't I?'

★ ★ ★

Tuesday morning's downpour was more Niagara Falls than April showers. Fiona peered out of her bedroom window and thought how fortunate she was to be indoors on such a wet morning.

She wondered if such horrible weather might deter the new client from keeping his appointment then told herself it was pointless worrying about something that mightn't happen.

But by half-past ten, sunshine filtered through the slats of her window's Venetian blind, and having checked at least three times that her hair was tidy and she didn't have lipstick on her teeth, she decided it was too late to run away and that she was, if not exactly looking forward to her first client meeting, as ready as she'd ever be.

51

Visitors to number 7 Lavender Lane were faced with a discreet notice inviting them to take the stairs to the first floor and ring the bell on the door facing them. The ground floor was occupied by a firm of solicitors during business hours Monday to Friday and every Saturday morning.

Fiona hadn't yet spoken to any of the staff but knew rent was paid regularly each month into her business account. This gave her some comfort if she let herself worry whether she could make a go of her business.

She was standing in the doorway of the tiny kitchen beside her assistant's office, wondering whether to switch the kettle on, when the shrill ring of the bell outside made her jump. How silly was that? Hadn't she been waiting for the new client to arrive?

If indeed it was the pilot, of course, and not someone wanting legal advice but who'd missed the solicitor's sign. That happened now and then.

'Come in,' she called, smoothing an

imaginary crease from her dark grey pencil skirt which she wore with a snow-white cheesecloth shirt.

A man, several inches taller than her and with broad shoulders and a commanding air, came through the door and looked enquiringly at her.

Fiona gulped and managed a weak smile.

'Mrs Maple?'

For the first time, she realised that people who didn't know her would assume she was Mrs Maple herself. Maybe that wasn't such a bad thing . . .

Her new client closed the door behind him and strode forward.

'Pleased to meet you. I'm Tim Carlisle. I hope I'm not too early.'

'Um, no,' she croaked. Pull yourself together, she thought. Just because her new client was an extremely attractive man who made her think of Robert Redford was no reason for acting like a lovestruck teenager. What on earth was he doing here?

'Let me take your coat.' The best she

could come up with.

'Thanks.' He removed his smart trench-coat and gestured to the stand in the corner. 'I'll hang it there, shall I? It shouldn't drip water on your floor because I took a taxi from Paddington Station.'

'Er, good. If you'd just like to come through to my office and make yourself comfortable . . . Would you like a hot drink?'

'No, thank you. I'd sooner get on with the business in hand.'

Putting her in her place? Fiona couldn't help feeling ruffled as she led the way.

'What beautiful prints.' He didn't sit down in the most comfortable chair she could find, but stood gazing at the pictures on the wall. 'This French café scene is particularly pleasing,' he said. 'Is Paris a favourite haunt of yours?'

'No, actually I inherited these pictures.' She cleared her throat, reluctant to admit she'd only ever left the country for one holiday in Spain.

Nor did she intend telling him she

was about to conduct her very first client interview. Maybe if I sit down, he'll follow suit, she thought.

Trying her hardest to appear more relaxed than she felt, she smiled at him and picked up her pen.

'I'll check we have your name and contact details correct though my assistant is an extremely efficient young lady. If you decide to register with us, you may find yourself dealing with Katie — that's Mrs Katie Armstrong — as well as with me.'

He nodded, listening as she read out his name, date of birth, phone number and address, all the time keeping those cornflower blue eyes fixed on her. Whatever was the man doing, seeking the services of a matchmaker when he appeared to have so much going for him?

Fiona ploughed on.

'I appreciate some of the questions I shall ask you might seem a little intrusive, Captain Carlisle, but I hope you'll cooperate, as a fuller knowledge of a client is most helpful when looking to find a suitable match.'

'Why don't you come straight out with it?'

'Come straight out with um, what, Captain Carlisle?'

'Tim. Please call me Tim.'

'All right. And I'm Fiona.'

He nodded his head.

'Pretty name. But you're wondering why a thirty-two-year-old airline pilot should need to consult a marriage bureau when aircrew must surely be so sought after. Isn't that right?' He was looking amused.

Fiona felt like a little girl caught trying on her mum's lipstick.

'Um, well, yes, I suppose we did wonder about that.'

'Because a man in his position must have scores of names in his little black book? Apart from all those air stewardesses, the captain's dashing uniform must make every lady he meets swoon with desire?' He gave a little grunt of amusement.

Fiona looked down at her notes.

'Well, I don't happen to be interested in women who are swayed by the classic image,' he continued.

'That's the stuff of trashy romantic novels and drippy films where boy meets girl and they walk off into the sunset hand in hand.'

She wanted to laugh but couldn't help feeling indignant over his criticism of romantic novels.

'I don't happen to consider 'Jane Eyre', not to mention 'Pride And Prejudice', trashy,' she said as sweetly as possible.

'I think you know what I'm getting at. My career doesn't make it easy for me to plan a social life, what with late night arrivals and early morning departures. The weather also plays a part in wrecking my plans.'

'I understand. You wouldn't want to be matched with a young lady whose working hours were also, shall we say, erratic?'

'Affirmative.' He folded his arms across his chest. 'What else do you need to know?' He looked straight at her.

Challenging her.

Fiona checked her list and decided on a different tack.

'Why don't you tell me a little about yourself?'

He nodded.

'Born in Hampshire. Father's a farmer. My sister was fourteen when I arrived and she married a farmer's son when I was only six so I spent a lot of my childhood getting under my dad's feet and helping with the animals.'

She nodded encouragement.

'Sounds good.'

'My uncle took me to an air show when I was about eleven and from then on, all I wanted to do was fly aeroplanes. I didn't do too badly at school and when I joined the RAF, I realised my dream. I've been flying as a commercial pilot for four years now.'

'Hobbies? Sports? Do you enjoy London life?'

'Hobbies?' He gave a shout of laughter. Fiona cringed inwardly and tapped the end of her pen against her front teeth.

'I go for walks when I can. Sometimes in the middle of the night when I get back from a flight. Sometimes very early in the morning. That's when I like this city most.'

Fiona, trying to cross one knee over the other, hit her leg against the desk and said 'Ouch!' She was about to fire another question at him when he spoke.

'Must we sit opposite one another at this desk? I feel as though I'm up before the headmistress.' Those Robert Redford blue eyes were twinkling at her.

'You're welcome to move your chair, Mr, um, Tim, but it's easier for me to make notes, sitting where I am.'

He shrugged.

'Next question?'

'We need to know what kind of young woman you'd like to meet. It seems to me you need someone who's very understanding. Someone who wouldn't mind your frequent absences and who wouldn't be jealous of your lifestyle.

'We wonder whether you'd consider a fashion model? We have one young lady on our records who is about to retire from modelling and would like to meet a kindred spirit.'

Fiona found her comment cut short.

'That probably means she's reached the age of thirty-five,' Tim said, 'and her agent can't find her any more work.'

Fiona felt that slight irritation again, like a woolly vest scratching her tender skin.

'Goodness, I hope that's not the case. Anyway, thirty-five isn't out of your age range, surely?'

The pilot raised his eyebrows.

'Well, no, I suppose not. But I thought we'd agreed not to consider anyone who wasn't independent?'

'Correct. But my client is currently looking around for another job and hasn't yet decided what she wants to do.'

'Apart from find a husband . . .' He was smirking.

'And you're not here to find a wife?' For moments they glared at each other. 'I'm sorry, Captain Carlisle, but I'm now very confused as to why exactly you are here if it's not for us to help you find a suitable partner.'

* * *

Next morning, Fiona lost no time in telling Katie about the obnoxious and arrogant airline pilot.

'Honestly, Katie, he's so full of himself, he's lucky I didn't chuck something at him!'

'That bad, eh? Does that mean you threw him out?'

'Of course not. We need all the clients we can get, don't we? He did have the grace to apologise for his clumsiness and I managed to simmer down and ask him to describe his ideal girl.' Fiona was still taken aback by the similarity of his description to her own appearance and personality.

'Well done. Has he registered, though? That's the important bit.'

'Yes, he has.'

'Yippee!' Katie clapped her hands together. 'Have you come up with any

61

matches yet?'

'I thought we'd go for that former model. The captain's agreed to see her after the cooling off period. Rosemary Blake's her name.'

'I remember. I think that waiting time was an excellent idea of Millie's. Before then, she told me people sometimes registered, couldn't wait for an introduction, then complained that the first person we introduced them to wasn't at all what they'd expected.

'Allowing them time to think over what details they gave us is good, because they can always add something or ask for something else to be deleted.

'I once registered a woman who was allergic to cats but she forgot to mention it until we put a delightful man who bred Siamese cats in touch with her. They spoke on the telephone and she liked the sound of him but he couldn't possibly give up his occupation and she'd have lived a miserable life if she'd settled down with him.'

'I can see the importance of dealing

with this kind of stuff before a couple meet,' Fiona said.

'It's our job to smooth the rocky road to love, is what your great-aunt used to say to me! Now, we might as well get out the card for the client you have in mind for Captain Carlisle and see how the two compare.'

'I did take a quick look but then the phone rang and another hopeful young lady walked in so I took her details. I meant to tell you but I keep on thinking back to the pilot and wishing I'd made a better job of interviewing him.'

'I shouldn't fret. He's registered so he can't think we're too bad. I need to refresh my memory about the model.' Katie pulled out the top drawer of the filing cabinet containing the files on clients currently hoping to find that special someone.

'What we must achieve, Fiona, is a state of professionalism. We're in a complicated business simply because our assets are human beings, often quite vulnerable and not sure whether they're doing the right thing.'

'That pilot's certainly not vulnerable,' Fiona muttered.

'Really? Are you quite sure?'

Fiona stared back at Katie.

'Well, I . . . he comes over as very much in control. He strikes me as being rather superior and I get the impression he's used to people obeying his every command.'

'Maybe so, but when he set foot in your office, he was out of his comfort zone and that's why he came over as arrogant.

'He's used to being the boss when he's in charge of an aeroplane, but to us, he's just another client. Except we have to make each one of them think they're the most important person in the world.'

'I'm learning such a lot.' Fiona pulled a wry face.

'And I'm still learning,' Katie said. 'What we must try for is not to become emotionally involved with clients. It's much better for all concerned if we managed to remain aloof.'

'Emotionally involved? Honestly, Katie, Girl Guide's honour, I can assure you I definitely haven't fallen for Captain Carlisle!'

Something to Report

The morning sped by, punctuated by phone calls, mostly from clients fretting over when they might hear about their next matches. At least two ladies complained they'd been waiting rather a long time, and Fiona, after promising to get back to both of them, had scanned the men currently on the list of hopefuls and found it sadly brief compared to the number of young women.

One of these was Rosemary Blake, the glamour girl. Fiona was crossing her fingers that she and the snooty pilot would hit it off.

'I've been thinking, Katie. What if we run an advertising campaign?' She looked up as her assistant brought her a cup of coffee.

'That can be expensive.' Katie folded her arms.

'How about you bring your coffee through so we can talk about it?'

Fiona jotted a couple of ideas on her

notepad before Katie sat down opposite.

'My turn to make the next round of drinks. I don't like to think you're waiting on me.'

'I shan't complain.' Katie grinned. 'Come on then, boss. What kind of marketing plan do you have in mind?'

'Nothing low-key like postcards in newsagents' windows. We have to be upmarket and modern. How about we contact the local paper?'

'We've advertised in their personal columns now and then and we ran a piece in a London evening paper a while back. Shall I set up another one?'

'Not for the moment, thanks. I'm thinking more about them running a story about us. Something less impersonal, aimed at readers learning more about what we actually do and how much we care about helping people find happiness.'

Katie nodded.

'When I pop out for lunch, I could bring back a paper. The local rag comes out today.'

'That would be great, thanks. If only we can persuade one of their reporters to interview us, that might help to get people talking about us.'

Katie's smile was wistful.

'Millie began in a very quiet way, making her services known to friends who spread the word. But that was a different era. I think she'd approve of your idea, Fiona.'

'Oh, I do hope so! We have to remember a lot of people are unhappy with their lot nowadays. According to Dad, since the Swinging Sixties, Britain's been marking time and no-one really knows what to expect. He thinks this is a strange decade.'

'Is that why so many people are looking to emigrate?'

'I imagine so. I read in the Sunday paper that more people are leaving than arriving.'

Katie shrugged.

'My mum says she and Dad are better off nowadays. They've bought a colour TV as well as a hostess trolley because they like to invite people over.'

'A hostess trolley? I don't think my mother would know what to do with one of those.'

'It wouldn't appeal to me but Mum's delighted with hers. Do you have any more ideas for improving the business? I don't really fancy walking round wearing a sandwich board.'

'Perish the thought! No, I don't think we'll go to those lengths, Katie. Maybe I'll look at the cost of advertising in a women's magazine, but not one of those expensive glossies. How about one that's more middle-range?'

'That's not a bad idea. We can't compete with the marriage bureaux in Mayfair, except by offering lower fees. But if we can become better known in this area and, dare I say it, around Britain in general, we'd have more chance of attracting new clients.'

'It's definitely worth a try.'

The doorbell rang and Katie shot to her feet.

'No appointment booked so maybe it's

a new inquiry. Perhaps we'll end up having more clients than we can cope with?'

★ ★ ★

Two days later, Fiona pushed open the door of the premises occupied by 'Park News'. The outer office was so cramped, the poor receptionist needed to watch her left elbow every time she hit the carriage return on her typewriter. She paused, both hands suspended above the keyboard and gave Fiona a big smile.

'Can I help?'

'I hope so. Is it possible to speak to one of your reporters about my business?'

'Do you want to place a small ad? I have a list of charges here.' She reached for a black leather folder.

Fiona shook her head.

'Thanks, but what I'm really after is being featured in your newspaper so that people who don't bother with the advertisements section might read about our services. The work we do is very interesting.'

The girl looked unconvinced.

'You can leave your name and telephone number if you like.' She pushed a memo pad across the counter and rummaged for a pen.

Fiona felt a huge wave of disappointment. Somehow, she must encourage this young woman to want to help her. She peered at the girl's hands and saw she was wearing a small diamond engagement ring.

Fiona wrote down her name and phone number.

'Thanks, but could I ask you something?'

'Of course.'

'How did you meet your fiancé?'

The receptionist giggled.

'That's a funny question. I met him on a blind date with my girlfriend and her boyfriend.'

'How lovely! The only blind date I ever went on was a nightmare. My bloke didn't stop talking about motorbikes all evening.'

'Oh, poor you. But why did you want

to know how I met my fiancé?

'Because I run a marriage bureau and I want to help people who aren't as fortunate as you and your young man to find happiness.'

'Gosh. I'm not sure if we've ever run a story like that before.'

Fiona was about to say there was always a first time, when a young man appeared in the doorway through to what looked like a big, inner office.

'Good morning,' he said. 'Did I hear the words 'marriage bureau'?'

Roddy Mitchell was a happily married man who'd met his wife when he'd been at college and the idea of wedded bliss hadn't even entered his head. He admitted to having previously been uninterested in how people found romance, but to Fiona's delight he agreed to visit Lavender Lane next day at noon.

★ ★ ★

The girls agreed that Katie would greet Mr Mitchell on arrival. She showed him

72

into the boss's office in the hope that this would create a good impression. He'd brought his notebook along and was happy for Fiona to explain to him how the bureau operated.

'If you want to know more about the years when my great-aunt ran the business, I'll hand you over to my assistant.'

'I don't have too much page room so we'll keep to the essentials. Could you start by telling me what kind of person you hope to attract?'

Fiona needed no further encouragement.

'We're here for anyone who longs to find someone they can get on with, feel at home with and possibly fall in love with.

'Our clients come from varied backgrounds and many different professions and trades. We have a number of widows and widowers looking for a second chance at happiness, as well as bachelors and spinsters, of course.'

He was scribbling furiously.

'What's your success rate?'

She gulped.

'I don't have the exact figures handy but I can assure you there have been many matches made. It's a very rewarding business to be involved in and you can imagine how thrilling it is when a couple decide to marry.'

He nodded and went on to enquire about fees. Fiona tactfully skirted round this by saying that was a matter for discussion with the individual concerned. She thought the registration fee was too low but that wasn't her concern just then.

'So many young people used to meet at church socials or tennis clubs and dance halls. Even though there are many more women in the workplace these days, often they have little chance of meeting the right kind of man.'

Roddy looked up and grinned.

'What is the right kind of man?'

'A gentleman,' she said firmly. 'Whether he's a plumber, a politician or a postman doesn't matter. Everyone who registers with the bureau puts their trust in us. So, we try to ensure that men and women who confide their personal details are both respectable and entitled to be introduced to another respectable man or woman.'

He nodded.

'That sounds fair enough. Any juicy stories?'

'Goodness! Katie can probably think of one or two as she's worked here longer than I have.'

'So why are you in charge, Mrs Maple?'

She let that pass.

'Please call me Fiona. I've been lucky enough to inherit the bureau from a relation. Already I love the work and very much enjoy meeting so many delightful people.' Don't think about the pilot, she told herself. She sat back in her chair.

'Well, well. Tucked away down Lavender Lane is a place where those who are lonely and looking for love may well find a pot of gold when they climb the stairway to paradise.'

'That's a bit flowery,' Fiona suggested.

'If you say so.' Roddy closed his notebook. 'I'll do the best I can for you,

Fiona. I've enjoyed our chat.' He smiled and rose to his feet.

She stood up too, holding out her hand for him to shake.

'I appreciate you taking the trouble to visit us, Roddy, and I look forward to reading your feature. Now, let me see you out.'

She walked him through to the reception room and closed the door behind him. Katie emerged from her office at once. 'How did it go?'

'Not sure. He asked me if I could tell him any juicy stories but I got around that.'

'Is he doing a feature on us?'

'On the business, yes. We have to wait and see what happens next, don't we?'

A Match Made in Heaven?

What happened next was a visit from Miss Rosemary Blake. Katie let her in.

'How lovely to see you,' she said. 'Would you like to talk to Fiona or may I help?'

'I'd like to meet the new owner but I'd like you to be there as well, as you interviewed me.'

'Do sit down and I'll pop through to the other office.'

Katie tapped on Fiona's door and put her head round it.

'Sorry to interrupt but Rosemary Blake wants a word with both of us. Is that OK with you?'

'Of course. It'll be good to meet her.'

Fiona got to her feet as the glamorous client entered her office.

'How do you do, Miss Blake? Come and sit down.'

'I'm very well, thank you, Miss Maple.'

'Please call me Fiona.'

Miss Blake raised her beautifully

groomed dark eyebrows. Fiona imagined her standing beside the annoying but attractive airline pilot and decided theirs would either be a match made in heaven or the other place.

'So, you're the one who's in the driving seat? Well, I was sorry to hear about Mrs Maple but of course I never met her. Katie told me you'd be taking over. I hope you're enjoying London.'

'I haven't seen much of it yet, but I love being here, yes.' Fiona hesitated. 'I imagine you have something important you'd like to discuss?'

'I was coming into town anyway so it seemed sensible to drop in. I'm still working but my contract ends very soon.' She looked down at her hands.

'Oddly enough, when I told you what kind of things I was hoping for in a husband, I refused to confirm whether I was interested in having children. Now, having thought very hard, I'd like you to alter my details so any possible suitors know what they're in for.'

'Well, that's good news.' Fiona glanced

at Katie. 'We've only provided one introduction for Miss Blake so far, haven't
we?'

'That's right. And we have at least one
more possibility though we can't say for
sure at the moment.'

'The shy librarian was very pleasant but I'd need to give him a complete
change of wardrobe and stop him light-
ing up that dreadful pipe.' She chuckled.
'What about this other possibility?'

'He's still in the cooling off period
as we call it. I'll be contacting him very
soon,' Katie added.

'Dare I ask what his occupation is?'

Katie glanced at Fiona.

'Excuse me,' she muttered and walked
over to the filing cabinet.

'Our new client is an airline pilot,'
Fiona said and flinched at Rosemary
Blake's peal of laughter. 'Um, would that
be a problem for you?'

'I'm not sure. Let's just say, pilots are
like all men, some are good and some
aren't. I'd be interested in meeting him.'

'Excellent.' Fiona was admiring the

way Rosemary Blake managed to wear a chocolate brown mini dress with such flair.

Having that coppery hair and those long legs must help. How wonderful it would be if their client fell in love with the pilot and he felt the same about her.

'We're hoping for a new influx of clients soon, Rosemary,' she said. 'The local paper has promised to publish a feature about us and I'm looking to gain publicity in one or two magazines.'

'Not just women's magazines, I hope.' The model smoothed her immaculate hair.

'Um, no, I take your point.' Fiona bit her lip. She really needed to do more research.

Katie rescued her.

'We have several farmers looking to find the right person. Would a more rural way of life appeal to you, do you think?'

'It might. But I'm not keen on travelling out of town to meet someone at this moment.'

'We understand,' Fiona said. 'Shall we

wait to see whether the airline pilot registers? If so, we'll contact you with his details and then the rest is up to you.'

'I'm happy with that,' the visitor agreed. 'At least he should have more to talk about than the dear little librarian.'

* * *

Timothy Carlisle had cold feet, though he couldn't help thinking that expression was an odd one. That night, after gliding down the flight path to another smooth landing at London Heathrow, he completed the formalities then headed to the car park and home.

Home was a flat far enough away from the airport to avoid most of the aeroplane noise without taking too long to drive to and from work. He loved his job but found his off-duty hours not so satisfying. And he was fed up with living alone, though his cooking skills had improved since he left the RAF where he'd eaten in the Officers' Mess with everything provided.

Sometimes he visited his parents in Hampshire and called on his sister whose two children were now teenagers. It was always good to see his folks but he'd drifted away from his former RAF mates except for one chap who he saw sometimes but who was happily settled down with a lovely young wife.

Seeing their happiness was what had really prompted Tim to contemplate contacting a marriage bureau — not that he'd told them that.

He hadn't told anyone at all, least of all the other pilots who worked for the same airline. They'd probably think he was crazy when there were so many attractive air stewardesses to ask out.

But he didn't relish the possibility of being gossiped about and worst of all, what if he was turned down? Also, his mother meant well, but she'd begun asking whether he had any thoughts of settling down. If she only knew . . .

But since his appointment with the attractive young woman who introduced herself as Fiona Maple, he'd somehow been transformed into an awkward adolescent again. How could that be? Fiona Maple was obviously a married lady, though come to think of it, he hadn't noticed a ring on her finger. But while eagle-eyed while flying, he could be very unobservant regarding the everyday things of life.

To make matters worse, he'd been feeling strangely unsettled. Except when on duty of course, when he could concentrate totally on flying the awesome jumbo jet he so enjoyed steering through the skies. He was in his element then. Confident. Relaxed. And happy as a pig in muck, as his dad would say.

How many miles had he flown since that momentous interview? Here he was, standing by his telephone again, about to ring to discuss his registration. He was in two minds about this.

The airline he worked for was about to take over another, smaller company. There'd be more routes to discover. More miles to fly. New people to meet. He mustn't delay any longer.

Tim picked up the phone, dialled the number, heard the voice of the pleasant-sounding young lady who worked with Mrs Maple, and explained his reason for calling.

* * *

'Yippee!' Katie bounced into the big office where Fiona sat shuffling index cards around on the desk's shiny surface.

'What are you so pleased about?' Fiona sat back in her chair.

'Tell me what you're up to first. Can anyone play?'

Fiona chuckled.

'I'm grouping like-minded clients together and trying to unravel thoughts that have been nagging at me. Come on, explain yourself, Mrs Armstrong.'

'He's decided to join us! Captain Charming is officially on our books!' Katie frowned.

'Oh, do pick your jaw up off the floor, boss. Even if you weren't sure, I didn't for one moment think you'd put him off

84

the idea of marriage.'

Fiona moved a pink card giving details of a female PE teacher with a phobia about water alongside a blue card holding information on a merchant navy skipper wanting a wife who'd sail with him. Katie noticed the error, giggled, then collapsed into the chair opposite her boss.

'What's the matter?' Fiona asked.

Her assistant pointed to the cards.

Fiona knew she was blushing.

'I . . . I probably have too much going around in my head. Anyway, though I wouldn't exactly describe Captain Carlisle as a charmer, his acceptance is excellent news, Katie. Will you contact Rosemary Blake?'

'Of course. And that red-headed girl who works in the big store in Oxford Street is another possibility for Captain Handsome Pants. Her dream is to see more of the world.'

'Good stuff, Katie. I take it you've looked at the pilot's photograph?'

'You bet. I like the fact that he hasn't

provided a picture of himself in uniform as I suspect some chaps might have.'

'That's true. I noticed his star sign is Aquarius — totally the wrong one for me. But then I'm not looking for a husband.'

Katie gave her a very appraising stare.

'I'd better get back to work.' Fiona looked down at the cards again.

'I'll leave you in peace, then. Are you sure you're not sickening for something?'

'I've been sitting up at night doing a lot of reading lately. But I'm fine, Katie, really I am.'

'You know what they say about all work and no play? I'd best go and make that phone call. I think our Miss Blake's going to be one happy lady.'

★ ★ ★

Katie tried several times but without success to speak to Miss Blake on the telephone. She'd left the office for lunch when Fiona picked up a call.

'Fiona? It's Rosemary Blake. I've

been out all morning but I heard my phone ringing as I got out of the lift. I wondered if you were trying to reach me — my friends and family always ring in the evenings.'

'Yes, Katie was trying to get in touch with you. Our client, Timothy Carlisle, would very much like to meet you, Rosemary.'

'Really? Well, I look forward to my second introduction. Remind me, please. What happens next?

'If you give us permission to pass your telephone number to him, or if you prefer, just your postal address, we'll do that today. Then the ball's in your court.'

'Let me see . . . Oh, I tell you what. If you don't reach him by phone today, could you pop my address and telephone number in the post, please?

'I'm free for the next few days before I have my final bookings with the agency. You never know, he might be off duty, too. I'm so looking forward to meeting this chap.'

'That's good to hear.' Fiona tried to

sound cheerful. Maybe I need a tonic, she thought.

'Then I'll leave the matter in your capable hands.' Rosemary rang off.

Fiona decided to try Tim Carlisle's number immediately. She was surprised when he answered on the second ring, clearly stating his status and name.

'Captain Carlisle, this is Fiona Maple.'

'Oh, hello, Mrs Maple. Sorry, I was expecting a call from my flight briefing people.'

'I won't keep you. I'm calling to say Miss Rosemary Blake's happy for you to contact her. Do you have paper and pen handy?'

'Of course. I'm ready.'

For sure he was. He was calm and efficient and . . . Swiftly she read out the contact details and he repeated them to her.

'Well, I hope you have an enjoyable meeting with Miss Blake, Captain.'

'I wish you'd call me Tim. But thanks anyway. I . . . I wish it could be . . .'

'I'm sorry?'

'Look, I mustn't keep you any longer. Thanks again and I'll report how I get on.'

She replaced the receiver. All of a sudden, she knew exactly what must be wrong with her. It had to be loneliness. Why hadn't she realised this before? She put so much energy and enthusiasm into her new job, she'd forgotten how to have fun.

In fact, she hadn't had all that much fun when she'd been seeing Daniel. So much had happened since the night they'd decided they were going nowhere together and now she was left feeling as though she'd gone through a wringer.

That would explain why she'd begun having very odd dreams, most of them involving aeroplanes.

* * *

Timothy Carlisle arrived at the arranged meeting place ten minutes early. The hotel foyer wasn't crowded so he chose a table for two not far from the entrance and informed a hovering waiter that he was awaiting a friend.

The moment Rosemary Blake walked through those revolving doors and into the foyer, he recognised her from her description and got to his feet. She smiled as he approached.

'Captain Carlisle?'

He held out his hand for her to shake.

'Please call me Tim. May I call you Rosemary?'

'Of course. I hope I'm not late.'

'Not at all. I arrived a little early. Shall I order some coffee or would you prefer something stronger?'

'Coffee's fine, thanks.'

'Let's go through to the lounge, shall we?'

'Why not?'

He steered her by her elbow, thinking how glamorous she was in her red and black long-sleeved mini dress. Some of the air stewardesses he knew were of the same mould as Rosemary Blake.

She must have enjoyed a lucrative modelling career, yet, for some reason he couldn't explain, he felt a little disappointed.

He told himself to pull himself together and enjoy the moment. After all, they might have masses of things in common, if only he could think of something interesting to say next.

A waiter darted forward and pulled out a chair for Rosemary who flashed him a brilliant smile. Tim sat down opposite her and gave their order while Rosemary took a powder compact from her handbag and checked her appearance.

'You look lovely,' he said, sitting back in his chair and crossing one leg over the other.

'Thank you, kind sir.'

He noticed her gaze move to his feet. She was looking a little surprised, as though something was disturbing her. He went hot and cold as he checked he hadn't put two odd shoes on that morning.

No, he was wearing his new dark brown loafers and a pair of canary-yellow socks that he thought looked rather far out, a description he'd heard his nephew and niece use when they were pleased with something. It couldn't be his footwear that bothered her, then.

'Um, I hear you're giving up modelling,' he said.

'That's right. My contract's about to come to an end and I feel like settling down.' He felt a moment of panic. 'Settling into something where I don't have to fly off to different places for modelling jobs. I think it's time for a change, so I'm job-hunting at the moment,' she said.

'Well, I hope you find the right position. What exactly did you have in mind?'

'Nothing to do with fashion, though should I marry, I wouldn't object to my husband being involved in it.'

'I notice you're a little bit older than I am.'

As soon as the words left his mouth, he knew they were a mistake. What had possessed him to say such a thing!

Rosemary's polite expression froze into one of contempt. Pointedly, she looked down at his feet and gave a little huff. Luckily, the waiter turned up and began putting the coffee pot and cups on the table before leaving them to it.

'I suppose you're waiting for me to serve you?' She was looking resigned.

'Not at all. Allow me.' Tim picked up the coffee pot and filled a cup right to the top.

'Thank you,' she said. 'It's a good job I take mine black.'

He topped up his cup with milk and tried to think of a film that was popular at the moment but with no success.

'I expect, like me, you don't find time to visit the cinema too often.' The words came out in a rush.

Rosemary shrugged.

'I prefer the theatre when I can get there. A friend mentioned going to see 'The Return Of the Pink Panther' but I don't think I can be bothered.'

They sat in silence for a while, Tim beginning to wonder why on earth he'd ever visited Mrs Maple's establishment in the first place. Rosemary was checking her watch and probably wishing the same.

It looked like the pilot and the soon to be unemployed model looking for a new career were definitely not destined to jump off the launch pad together.

* * *

Fiona was conducting an interview with a man who was planning a new life in Australia and who wanted to begin it by taking his bride with him.

'I see,' she said thoughtfully as the client stopped speaking and sat back in his chair.

'Well, do you think you can help?' He looked beseechingly at her.

She smiled.

'We'll do our best. Your requirement will reduce the number of suitable ladies, of course, but you're a very presentable gentleman, still in your early forties and you say you've inherited a fair sum of money from your late parents.'

'I don't earn an enormous salary as a teacher but I do want to teach once I've settled in. There's a lot to sort out but I have a friend over there advising me and I'm looking at Adelaide or thereabouts.

'My new wife wouldn't have to find a job but if she wanted to, I wouldn't stand in her way.'

Fiona cleared her throat. She still hadn't become used to asking what she considered to be questions of a delicate nature but she knew it was important to know exactly what her clients wanted out of life.

Hopefully, marriages made via Mrs Maple's Marriage Bureau would have the same chance of success as any made through people meeting by chance at a party or through their work.

'As I say, you have a lot to offer, but we'll have our work cut out to find someone prepared to leave her homeland. Another thing we need to know is whether you'd like to start a family in your new life. After a suitable interval, of course!'

'I'd certainly like to have children with the right girl. I'm not daft enough to expect a Hollywood type love match with a dewy-eyed young blonde. Someone in her mid-thirties would be my ideal choice. She doesn't have to be glamorous — indeed, I don't think I'd feel at home with a fashion plate.'

'Ah.' Fiona felt a surge of hope. There were several ladies on the books who fitted his description and often the gentlemen clients were looking to find a pretty twenty-something girl to show off like a trophy to their friends.

She jotted down a few notes and looked up.

'When would you hope to leave London?'

'Not until the New Year. I've arranged the school Christmas concert for years now — call me sentimental, but I'd like to do one final performance.'

Fiona was warming to him. She couldn't wait to begin searching the index cards in hopes of finding him a suitable young lady.

But they had no time to lose and he'd assured her he didn't want her to give him the seven-day cooling-off period. He taught in a secondary modern school and could reach the centre of London easily by bus or Tube.

After Fiona saw her client to the door, assuring him they'd be in touch soon, Katie looked up from her work.

'How did that go?'

'Very well. He's easy-going over the way a young woman should look and sensible about age, but he's expecting a lot!' Briefly she explained the situation.

'That's a wonderful opportunity for someone though, isn't it?' Katie said.

'He strikes me as a nice man who's been living a quiet life and now his windfall has given him the confidence to up sticks.

'Who have we got, Katie? I can only think of that young woman who cheerfully mentioned her thick ankles. I seem to recall her saying she'd happily move but whether she meant to another continent, I don't know.'

'I interviewed her.' Katie sounded triumphant. 'Miss Forbes is a primary school teacher and she might well be a good match, or at least have distinct possibilities. They're both very realistic about not having huge expectations. It's a pity more of our clients don't feel the same way.'

Fiona opened her mouth to speak just as someone knocked on the door. Before either of them could move, Rosemary Blake stormed through the door. She looked, Fiona decided, as though she'd just been sucking on a lemon.

Their glamorous client had rung the day before to confirm she planned to meet Captain Carlisle today at a suitable venue. Now Fiona was wondering whether he'd stood Rosemary up. She sucked in her breath and managed to produce her best, most reassuring smile.

Back to the Drawing Board

'I'm very glad you're both here,' Rosemary announced. 'I have just spent the most miserable half hour of my life with that awful man!'

'Let's go through to my office,' Fiona said quickly. 'Katie, will you come, too, please? Just so we both understand exactly what this is all about.'

What on earth could the pilot have done to incur so much discontentment?

Ignoring Katie's eye-rolling, doubtless because she was keen to look up contact details for the girl they were considering for Mr Jackson, Fiona leaped to open her door before their furious client could burst through it like a gale-force wind. Rosemary's usual calm, confident manner had plainly deserted her.

Their client sat down on the chair facing Fiona's desk. Fiona slid into her place and Katie perched on the wide window-sill with her back to London's lovely summer's day. The open Venetian blind allowed sunlight to stream into the room and the bunch of pink and white stocks Fiona had bought from a nearby flower stall filled the room with their sweet fragrance.

'Now, what seems to be the problem?' Fiona asked gently.

Rosemary Blake's answering snort was anything but gentle.

'The man's an idiot. When I first saw his photo, he reminded me of Robert Redford and he didn't disappoint in real life. At least not then,' she said darkly.

'To be fair, he arrived early, so I didn't have to wait on my own and he was perfectly polite at first. But after coffee was served, I couldn't help noticing the ghastly, bright yellow monstrosities he was wearing . . .'

She paused for dramatic effect.

'I could probably try to change his taste in socks — and ties for that matter — but worst of all, he pointed out that I was older than him. What a nerve! At that moment,' she said in a stage whisper, 'I knew we weren't on the same wavelength and never could be.'

Fiona blinked hard.

'Oh, dear, I'm so sorry, Rosemary. Perhaps he was nervous.' Why was she making excuses for him?

'Huh! I have an awful suspicion he hides behind his smart uniform with its four gold rings on the jacket sleeve. In real life, he needs whipping into shape, if you want my honest opinion. Please find me someone else,' she pleaded. 'This has been such a disappointment.'

Katie, who'd been keeping a low profile, got to her feet.

'No problem,' she said. 'We'll give the matter our urgent attention and be in touch as soon as possible.'

'Absolutely.' Fiona nodded her head. 'Katie, I wonder about the doctor who registered recently. He's Home Counties, widowed and too busy to socialise. Rosemary, how does that sound to you?'

'Well,' Rosemary said, 'I like the thought of becoming a doctor's wife and I'm sure I could manage his calendar better than he does. How old is this man? No more chaps who are younger than me, please, ladies!'

'I believe he's just turned forty-five,' Katie said.

Rosemary Blake uncrossed her slender nylon-clad legs and stood up.

'How tall?'

'Over six feet, from memory, but I can easily check.' Katie opened the filing cabinet and began riffling through folders.

Fiona rose too and smiled reassuringly.

'My assistant's recall of clients is admirable. I have another gentleman in mind who might well suit you too, so please don't lose heart. And, who knows, the medical man could well be your Dr Right!'

'Let's hope this one's my third time lucky.' Rosemary checked her watch. 'I have an appointment with my dressmaker soon, but you can contact me later.'

With that, she turned and sailed out of the door like a film star parading the red carpet. Fiona and Katie exchanged glances as they heard the sound of high heels clicking down the linoleum-covered stairs and Katie put her hand to her mouth, obviously suppressing a fit of the giggles.

'She's so bossy,' Fiona whispered.

'Isn't she just?' Katie whispered back. 'Yellow socks? What is her problem?'

'I know. But should I have a word with him, d'you think?'

Katie shrugged. Moments later they heard the front door slam.

'Those poor people in the solicitor's office,' Fiona said. 'I shouldn't be surprised if their windows were rattling.'

'Their clients are usually very quiet, aren't they? Do you see much of your tenant?' Katie asked.

'Mr Wentworth and I hardly ever meet, even though we live in the same building. I've met his secretary, Jane, once or twice. She seems very pleasant.'

'Ideal folk to have as neighbours. Your great-aunt chose well.'

'Mr Wentworth certainly seems to be

103

a very nice person.'

Katie looked thoughtful.

'I wonder if he's looking for a wife.'

'Well, he knows where to come if he is! Now, I thought you were going to look up those contact details on the primary teacher? I'll get in touch with the doctor.'

'If I recall correctly,' Katie said, 'Helen Forbes should get back from school by five o'clock. I'm feeling quite excited for her!'

★ ★ ★

In next day's post, Fiona found a hand-written envelope addressed to her. Often clients who preferred to write rather than telephone, sent their letter to whichever of the two matchmakers had interviewed them. On this occasion, Fiona had been contacted by Captain Carlisle, before he set off for his next flight to New York.

'Dear Mrs Maple, You may have heard from Miss Blake that our first meeting didn't go too well. I apologise if I upset her in any way, but to be honest, I found her rather tedious. She seemed to take offence very easily and she also appeared to take a dislike to my shoes, for some unknown reason. I don't think either of us is in favour of a second date.

'It would be rather nice to meet someone a few years younger than me. It's not that Miss Blake is that much older, it's just that she makes me feel like a naughty schoolboy. That never, ever happens while I'm at work.

'I'll be away for the next four nights. Do you think you could sort out someone else for me to meet on my return? I don't mean to whine, but life can get a little lonely for a chap like me. Kind regards, Tim'

Fiona put the letter down on her desk blotter. Lonely? At this point in her life, she knew exactly what he meant. She loved her new career but spent a lot of time working and when she wasn't working, she was quite often planning and wandering back down to the office to check one client's details against those of another.

Katie had commented on her employer's solitary lifestyle, and Fiona realised she was experiencing the kind of situation many of her clients were trying to escape.

But she'd been trying to find her feet business-wise, also to settle into the neighbourhood. The local shop owners knew her by name now, but the only person anywhere near her own age was Katie, and she came in on the bus from Clapham every morning and didn't seem inclined to remain in the city in the evenings.

Fiona must decide which of her young lady clients might appeal to Tim Carlisle. She began looking through the index cards and exclaimed in triumph when she came upon a young widow now aged twenty-nine, then groaned as she saw this client longed to remarry and move from London.

Maybe true love would change the widow's mind? That thought brought her no joy whatsoever but she would telephone the client that evening and, if she approved, would write to Tim next day.

But the more she thought about it, the more she thought Rosemary might have a point regarding those socks.

*   *   *

'Office pranksters and attention seekers — that's my mum's opinion of men who wear yellow socks!' Katie called to her boss as she arrived next morning.

Inside her office, Fiona burst out laughing.

'Is that common knowledge or did your mum make it up?'

Katie appeared in the doorway.

'It's something she was told to look out for, like grubby fingernails or a man walking on the inside of the pavement when he's escorting you.'

'My goodness, what other horrors did she come up with?'

'Things like turning up late outside the cinema or expecting the girl to go halves on a first date. Oh, and driving to your house but staying in the car and honking the horn instead of ringing the doorbell.'

Fiona gestured to the letter before her.

'I'm writing to our dashing young pilot and wondering if I should put a PS recommending him not to wear those yellow monstrosities again.'

'Rather you than me. As a matter of interest, why are you writing by hand, not typing it?'

Fiona shrugged.

'I thought it might have more impact. I'm suggesting that young widow you interviewed as a possible. I rang her last night and she likes the idea.'

'Good, but doesn't she want a new life somewhere else?'

'I asked her about that,' Fiona said, 'but she's willing to meet with Tim Carlisle and both of them seem to want to get on with things.'

'They do indeed. And she's younger than he is so he can't go putting his yellow foot in it this time!'

'Let's hope not, anyway. Is that the

local paper you've got there?'

Katie handed it over.

'I had a quick peep and Roddy's feature's in there. Shall we take a look?'

'You bet!'

Fiona groaned as she read the headline: 'Finding True Love in Lavender Lane'.

'Don't you like it? I think it's OK.'

'It's all right. I suppose they have to go for eye-catching stuff.' Fiona began scanning the first paragraph and as each finished reading the article, they exchanged glances.

'Would this encourage you to consult Mrs Maple's Marriage Bureau?' Fiona asked.

'Yes, I don't see why not.'

'Hmm,' Fiona mused. 'Roddy goes on a bit about our ages. Why are newspapers so obsessed with how old a person is?'

'I don't know,' Katie replied. 'He talks about this brave enterprise — two young women on a mission to bring love into the lives of lonely men and women.' She wrinkled her nose. 'But they're not all lonely, are they? For a start, most of them are working.'

Fiona bit her lip and turned her gaze to the fat white pottery vase of flowers.

'Oh, gosh, I shouldn't have said that.' Katie reached for her friend's hand and gave it a quick squeeze. 'I truly didn't think. Loneliness comes in different ways, doesn't it? I miss my husband terribly but I can't say I'm lonely, working with you and going home to my parents each evening.'

'The weird thing is, Katie, it only occurred to me recently how similar my own situation is to that of many of our clients.'

'Maybe we should register you, then?' Katie almost whispered. 'Please don't think I'm being insensitive, Fiona.'

Fiona shook her head.

'We have enough trouble with awkward clients without creating any more embarrassing moments.'

* * *

'I'm afraid it's me again.'

Fiona knew at once who was ringing. She'd even heard that voice calling her in one of her aeroplane dreams, none of which she dared confess to Katie.

'Good afternoon, Captain . . . um, I mean Tim. And by the way, we pride ourselves on being at the end of a line in case a client needs to consult us. Now, how did your evening out go?' And why had her mouth gone dry?

'Not so well. I felt as though I was being interrogated. It was like the worst kind of interview when you know the interviewer's trying to trip you up. She hardly stopped talking all through the meal, mostly about what a wonderful person her late husband was and how she'd never be able to replace him.'

'Some would say that was a good thing — to let her talk about him, I mean. Are you sure you weren't a little bit on the defensive? Could you not give her another chance now she's got all that off her chest?'

He answered without hesitation.

'Absolutely and utterly not. She's an attractive young lady and I'm truly sorry she's been widowed so young, but there was no spark between us. And she didn't smile at me with her eyes.'

He sounded glum. Fiona felt herself wishing she could give him a hug and make him a nice cup of tea. What was she thinking of?

'Well, if you're quite sure, then we'll look at another prospect.'

'That sounds so cold-blooded, somehow. I wish . . . '

'Sorry, what do you wish?'

'Oh, nothing. I should apologise for being so pernickety.'

'You're entitled to be choosy. This isn't like buying a new shirt, you know.' He chuckled. 'No, I'll go along with that. By the way, I have a week's leave due to me and I need to take it before the peak holiday season begins. Would that help you plan further, shall we say, candidates, for me to meet?'

'We certainly wouldn't recommend you meeting two or three young ladies one after another during the course of a week.'

'No, ma'am. Of course not, ma'am.'

'Are you poking fun at me, Captain Carlisle?'

'Of course not, Mrs Maple.'

Fiona almost corrected him but resisted the temptation.

'Might I ask you something, Tim?'

'Ask away.'

'What colour socks were you wearing when you met our widowed young client for dinner?'

* * *

'Badminton. I suddenly thought of it on the bus home yesterday.' Katie stood in Fiona's doorway, looking triumphant.

'Why? Do we have a client living there?'

'I mean the sport, not the place! We could look in the local paper to see if there's a club nearby, or there might be a card on the noticeboard in the corner shop.'

'Why this sudden interest?'

'I'm thinking of a hobby you could take up, something to help you meet people,' Katie said.

'Have you seen my hand/eye coordination? A film club would suit me better.'

'OK. Yes, I could imagine you discussing one of those arty films with a nice, bearded intellectual.'

'Must he have a beard?'

'What if he looked like Clint Eastwood except with whiskers?'

Fiona was trying to keep a straight face.

'I might make an exception, but Clint's in his mid-forties.'

Katie glanced at her watch.

'Whoops, sorry — I forgot to tell you the pilot's calling in about five this afternoon. He rang while you were on the phone earlier — said it was just to check on something you'd mentioned.'

Fiona swallowed hard.

'That'll be the socks. And don't smirk, Katie, those socks are actually quite important.'

'So it would seem! Will you deal with him?'

'I'd better, I suppose. Haven't you got Helen Forbes coming in after she finishes for the day?'

'I have and I'm hoping she'll be the bearer of glad tidings. She sounded cheerful when she rang.'

'Well, fingers crossed. And with those two new registrations since our newspaper feature, we have another potential match for the pilot, don't we?

'Come to think of it, he hasn't met the girl who works for the department store.'

'She seems to be as difficult to match as he does. But which new lady do you mean?'

'The single mum. She's bright and attractive, but she says it's difficult to meet men who don't mind her having a daughter and Captain Carlisle told us he wouldn't turn down a young lady just because she had a child.'

'He's actually very open-minded,' Fiona said.

'Definitely. Over the years, we've had

clients who don't approve of divorce. This particular one is definitely divorced but it's on the grounds of desertion.'

Fiona felt a pang of sympathy.

'Oh, poor girl, that's awful. How brave of her, wanting to try again. I imagine she's hoping to find a loving father for her little girl, as well as a nice husband for herself.'

'Well, when your favourite client comes in, you might double-check what he thinks.'

'D'you mean before or after we talk about socks? And what's this about him being my favourite client?'

Katie winked.

'You have a soft spot for him — come on, admit it!'

'I doubt he has the same feeling about me. Remember, he doesn't like bossy females.'

'Because you've criticised his taste in footwear? What if he tells you his sock drawer also contains pairs of orange and candy pink and purple ones?'

'Then he'll have to toe the line, won't he?'

Three's Company

Katie was in her office talking to Helen Forbes when the doorbell rang at five o'clock. Fiona smiled to herself as she went to let the caller in. Right on the nail! The pilot spent his working life trying to keep to schedules.

'Good afternoon. Please come through.'

How handsome he looked in his uniform. Fiona still sometimes pondered why he seemed to have difficulty in meeting eligible young women, but she saw his point. An impressionable young female could easily be swept off her feet by his glamorous appearance and his jet-setting lifestyle.

To him of course, it was a way of earning a living, though he realised his luck in being able to fulfil his boyhood ambition. He'd talked a little to her about delays experienced and hanging round airports and impersonal hotels, each one very much like the last one he'd checked out of with his crew.

'There's tea brewing. Would you care to join me?'

'That's very kind.' Tim followed her into her domain and looked around. 'For an office, it's a very pleasant room. Do you live over the shop?'

She chuckled.

'That's one way of putting it. Yes, there's a lovely flat on the top floor.' She needed to move the conversation on, before he asked what her husband did for a living, preferring not to let her personal circumstances enter the conversation.

'I'll pour the tea,' she said. 'Milk and sugar?'

'Just milk, please.' He was looking at one of Millie's beautiful pictures so hopefully not noticing the lack of a gold band on Fiona's wedding finger.

'Are you heading for Heathrow or are you on your way home?'

'Home.' He picked up his teacup. 'So, what's wrong with my socks?'

She couldn't help but smile.

'I'm sure they're fine but some people have strong feelings about their colour.'

He sipped his tea.

'Rosemary being one of them. I wondered why she was looking at my feet.'

'Yellow's maybe not the best of colours to wear when meeting someone for the first time. Perhaps you could choose a more muted shade like blue or green, or there's always black, of course.'

His lips twitched.

'Or even navy blue like my uniform ones.'

He hitched up one trouser leg to prove it.

'I'm only trying to help you, Tim.' She was dying to laugh.

'I wore dark brown socks with beige diamond patterns when I met my last prospect. Did she comment on those, I wonder?' He looked put out now.

'You have so many good qualities and you're also a man of the world so we wondered whether you'd like to meet up with a delightful young woman whose husband deserted her. She's divorced, with a daughter who's four years old.'

'Right . . . so, what do you think?'

'Me?' Fiona felt startled.

'Yes, you have all the information in your files. But can you look beyond that? Can you imagine me running around the park with this young woman and her little girl? Because that's what I'd need to do, isn't it? These two come as a package.'

'I thought you didn't have a problem with single mothers?'

'I don't. I'm just trying to see this particular match-up with a new pair of eyes.'

They each concentrated upon picking up their tea cup and drinking from it.

'If you really do want to know what I think . . . '

'Yes, I do,' Tim said.

'I think you'll find out whether you want to get to know this young mum better after you've been in her company for a while. You appear to be a very self-contained person and it'll take someone very special to capture your heart.'

'Crikey.'

'That's only my opinion. I don't pretend to be a psychologist but my business is to try to help you find happiness with a suitable partner.'

He nodded solemnly.

'Of course. Your business is well-respected. I made inquiries before contacting you. I'd better invite this young woman you have in mind to join me for tea, maybe. If she's agreeable of course.'

'I'll let you know after I've made sure she's happy for you to get in touch. Might I suggest just the two of you meet on this occasion? If you hit it off, you can always meet the little girl another time.'

He agreed but not with much enthusiasm. And after he left, Fiona found herself wishing she could run after him. And for the life of her she couldn't work out why.

* * *

That evening, Katie and Fiona went out for a meal together. Katie's parents were touring the Scottish Highlands and when Fiona invited her assistant to have supper with her, Katie suggested they visit the nearby Italian restaurant.

'Honestly, I'm happy to cook something for us,' Fiona said.

'I know you are, but it'll do you good to get out and about. Have you even thought about my idea yet?'

Fiona wrinkled her nose.

'I really don't fancy playing badminton. Maybe I'll try a film society, but while we're so busy, I'd rather curl up on the settee these evenings and watch television or read.'

'It's great that the business has perked up again. Getting Mrs Maple's bureau written up in the local paper was an excellent move. Well done.'

'It's also good to know we're being recommended. Tim Carlisle told me he'd made inquiries about us. His former flying instructor met his second wife through the bureau. They'd both been widowed and everything worked out beautifully for them.'

'How lovely! I don't remember that so I imagine Millie must have worked her magic on them before I came here.'

Fiona was locking the office door.

'Let's hope there's some magic around when my favourite client, as you call him, meets Jenny, the single mum.'

Katie began walking down the staircase.

'Aha!' The exclamation floated upwards. 'So, the pilot's willing to take a chance, is he? Good for him. I meant to ask you how he reacted to the fashion advice.'

'I think I made my point.'

'Jenny mightn't have a problem with colourful socks. Most women would consider him to be quite a catch, don't you think?' Katie said.

Fiona ignored that.

'I think we deserve a little celebration. Supper's on me tonight, Katie. Just a little thank you for all you do around here.'

'But I love my job, boss. You don't need to thank me.'

'Oh, I think I do.'

They stepped outside into the mild evening. Passers-by were heading home and at the junction of Lavender Lane with the main highway, red double-decker buses were stuck at the traffic lights, engines grumbling. As the girls walked on, so the sounds of honking and revving engines increased.

'Don't you find London noisy, after living in a small town?' Katie asked.

'Funnily enough, I don't. Hardly any traffic noise reaches the flat and if I go for a walk, I head to the park.' They were waiting to cross the road.

'And you're feeling pretty settled in by now. How many weeks has it been?'

'It's almost two months. I'm hoping my folks will visit one weekend soon. They can use my bedroom and I'll sleep in that little box-room if I can move some of the junk out.'

'There's a camp bed in there. I stayed one night when there was a train strike and I was worried about getting home and back next morning. Your great-aunt and I ate fish and chips out of the paper that night.'

'You were such a help to her and now you're helping me.'

'Lights are green, Fiona, let's go!'

They hurried across and Katie pointed

out the next turning.

'Luigi's is down here on the left.'

Fiona knew Katie liked this eating place and had visited it with her husband.

'How much longer before Tommy finishes his cruise?' she asked.

'Exactly seven weeks before he docks in Southampton. According to him, it's more like a prison than a cruise liner.' She grimaced. 'Of course, he's exaggerating. At least we're both saving up and we'll be able to think about where we'll live once he comes home.'

Fiona didn't like to think about running the bureau without this competent young woman's assistance.

'Maybe he'll find a job in London?'

'We'll have to see. Here we are then — I rang to reserve a table as they can get quite busy here.' She pushed open the door.

Fiona followed her inside. Katie greeted one of the waiters by name while a man, presumably waiting to be seated, turned to face her. To her astonishment she recognised him.

The man smiled hesitantly at Fiona.

'Good evening, Miss Maple. It seems that great minds think alike.'

'Hello, Mr Wentworth. Yes, my assistant recommended this place so here we are.'

He gave a wry smile.

'I made a spur of the moment decision to eat out this evening, but it seems I may have to wait a while for a table. It serves me right for not being more organised.'

'I'm very lucky to have inherited Katie with my great-aunt's business.'

Katie was beckoning Fiona who made her own spur of the moment decision.

'Look, you're very welcome to join us, Mr Wentworth. In fact, you'd be doing us a favour — as long as you don't mind me checking out the male point of view on a few things. Total discretion of course,' she added hastily.

He looked uncertain.

'Are you sure your assistant won't

mind? It's very kind of you. Outside of office hours, I lead quite a solitary life, to be honest.'

'Let me make sure.'

She headed for the table where Katie was waiting and whispered her request. Moments later, Mr Wentworth was on his way to join them. He waited for the waiter to make a fuss of Fiona then gratefully accepted the extra chair that appeared.

'This really is most civil of you,' he said. 'I hope you'll let me order a bottle of wine for the three of us to share.'

The girls looked at each other.

'I was going to order a carafe of house wine,' Katie said. 'But we can share a bottle, of course.'

'I'll make sure it's added to my bill,' he said. 'And please do call me Geoff, won't you?'

'Of course,' Fiona said, smiling up at the waiter bringing her a menu. 'You must've known Katie for a few years, and my name's Fiona.'

'Yes, indeed. But we've all tended to

keep ourselves to ourselves, I suppose.'

'You wrote me a very kind letter of condolence and I should have thanked you before.'

'I read it, too,' Katie chimed in. 'It was beautifully expressed.'

'The least I could do.' He looked at Fiona. 'Millie and I used to play Scrabble sometimes on a Saturday afternoon. Occasionally we'd both see clients who couldn't get away from work during the week and we'd play Scrabble, drink tea and eat custard creams.'

'I never realised that,' Katie said. 'But she was an intensely private person.'

'She was a real demon with the Scrabble tiles! I miss Millie very much, but I can see she left her beloved bureau in very capable hands.'

He broke off to order a bottle of Italian red wine. The girls concentrated on choosing their meals and soon the three of them were clinking glasses and drinking each other's health.

Geoff, who Fiona had considered to be a very timid sort of man possessed a dry sense of humour and was obviously longing to hear more about the girls' progress with the business.

'Quite frankly,' Fiona said as they began on their starters, 'I'd have floundered without Katie's help. I didn't take long to realise how invaluable she is to the bureau.'

'Nonsense,' Katie protested.

Geoff chuckled.

'You obviously get on well. Dare I ask if you've increased your client base since the local paper ran that feature?'

'It did help, yes,' Fiona replied. 'But I think Millie and Katie clocked up several successes just before I, um, entered the proceedings so there was a lull while things were sorted out.'

'We realise how important it is to have clients recommend our services. I imagine you find the same, Geoff?'

'Definitely. But my legal practice is very dry and dusty compared with your line of work.' He turned to Fiona. 'You said something about the male point of view? I'm happy to help if I can.'

Katie cleared her throat.

'That's a really kind offer. We do have a minor problem with one of our gentleman clients. This one has a determined view of what kind of socks he should wear.'

Fiona groaned.

'And I've had to discuss this with him. I think Katie received some feedback as well.'

Katie nodded.

'There was a comment about him wearing socks that make him look as if he'd just come from the golf course.'

'Well, perhaps he had,' Geoff said. 'My goodness, I didn't realise how fraught this whole business could be. I'm very out of touch with that kind of thing.'

'Would you be offended if you were in our client's position and your taste in clothes was criticised?'

'Ah, well, if I was intent on finding a wife and my choice of clothing was an obstacle to success, I'm sure I'd take note of the criticism!'

'And if you were meeting a lady for

the first time, would you mention the fact that she was a little older than you?'

'My goodness, no! That would really put the kybosh on things. My late wife was four weeks older than me and I used to tease her about it but she used to tease me about my terrible singing voice.' His face took on a tender expression.

'If two people love one another, they'll put up with little annoyances. If you really want to know what I think, it is that the ladies concerned were looking for reasons not to see this gentleman again.

'Maybe they didn't want to appear fussy so they were grasping at straws when they complained about colour co-ordination.'

'That's so interesting.' Fiona sat back as the main courses arrived and the waiters backed off again.

'It makes sense,' Katie agreed.

'I'm so sorry to hear about your wife, Geoff,' Fiona spoke softly.

'I didn't realise, either,' Katie said.

'It's been more than three years now.

Life changed dramatically for me, I'm afraid. But she'd be cross with me for not getting out and about more.

'We used to play badminton with a group.' He looked in amazement at the two girls as they began to chuckle. 'What have I said?'

'I'm so sorry. Please don't think we were being disrespectful!'

Fiona swiftly explained.

'If you really don't fancy the idea, it's pointless trying it, in my opinion,' Geoff said. 'But it really is time I did something about my personal situation. As I said, Nancy — that was my wife's name — she wouldn't have wanted me to spend the rest of my life alone. Nor do I want to end up a lonely old man.'

Fiona met Katie's gaze as Geoff sipped his wine.

'How would you feel about letting us help you meet someone? Not someone to replace Nancy, because that could never be. But someone who possesses some of the qualities that are important to you and who's maybe in the same position?'

'I'm rattling around on my own at home. Our son is in the army and currently on an overseas posting, so my life revolves around my practice. I commute an hour each way so I'm not at home much except at weekends. And I've given up taking holidays.

'My word, you've set me thinking now.'

The girls ate in silence. Fiona sensed he needed a little quiet time and when she caught Katie's eye, she knew she felt this too.

'How strange life is,' Geoff said at last. 'All those people walking up and down the stairs for their appointments and me in my office going about my day. It never, ever occurred to me that Mrs Maple's Marriage Bureau might be just the thing for me.'

★ ★ ★

'We'll see you to your door, Fiona,' Geoff said, after the bill was paid and they stood outside on the pavement. 'Then I can walk Katie to her bus stop on my way to the Underground station.'

As they arrived at number 7, Fiona took out her key and turned to the other two.

'Thanks for livening up my evening, both of you. We really must do this again.'

'I agree,' Geoff said. 'Being seen out with two such delightful young ladies will do wonders for my new image.'

'Such a flatterer!' Katie teased. 'I've had a lovely evening and I look forward to seeing both of you tomorrow.'

'I'll call in between appointments and book an interview,' Geoff said. 'And that's a promise.'

A New Recruit

Next morning, Fiona heard the phone ringing as she unlocked her office. Jenny, the young mum, lost no time in telling Fiona she'd arranged to meet Timothy Carlisle that afternoon for tea in one of London's famous department stores.

'My mother's going to look after my little girl,' she said. 'I thought it was best if I saw him on my own and he agreed. He sounds very charming.

'But what a strange life he must lead, flying all over the world.'

'Would that bother you?' Fiona found herself gripping the telephone receiver hard.

There was a pause.

'I don't think so. Probably I shouldn't think about what he does and concentrate on whether I like him as a person and, of course, whether he takes a liking to me.'

'How very wise.' Fiona couldn't help feeling wistful.

'I never thought I'd be contacting a marriage bureau but I hope I've made the right decision.'

'It's very normal for people to feel as you do, Jenny, but having chosen to trust in us, you can be certain we always try to suggest possible matches who fit at least some of the criteria we're given. Sometimes that's not so easy, but you certainly don't fit that category.'

'I'm quite a simple soul, really. That worries me a bit, considering what a glamorous life the captain must lead.'

'Please don't concern yourself with that,' Fiona said. 'He'll probably tell you certain aspects of his career are similar to what a bus driver does.'

Laughter gurgled down the line.

'He sounds as though he has a good sense of humour.'

'Yes, you're right about that.'

'And he's told me he won't be in uniform so I'm to look for a fair-haired, six-foot-tall man wearing a sports jacket with white shirt, stripy tie and light grey trousers. He'll wait for me outside the

136

entrance to the restaurant. Oh dear, my tummy's lurching at the thought of it. Has he seen my photograph, Fiona?'

'No, Jenny, he hasn't. A while back, we made a decision not to show clients each other's photographs unless someone absolutely insisted. Some people aren't particularly photogenic and others try too hard to smile or end up blinking just as the picture's taken. So far, it hasn't been a problem. I think my assistant mentioned your colouring and build to Captain Carlisle.'

'I mustn't keep you any longer. I'll let you know how it goes, shall I? How awful it would be if I liked him a lot and he didn't feel the same about me!'

'Jenny, try not to think too hard about what might or mightn't happen. I know it's easy for me to say but just try to relax and enjoy yourself.'

'I'll do my best. Thanks, Fiona.'

Within moments, Katie put her head round the door.

'Geoff's here and he'd like a word with both of us.'

'Oh, right. I'll come on through.'
Maybe he'd had second thoughts.

Geoff was standing in the waiting area, studying a pot plant in the window. He turned to greet Fiona and Katie.

'Good morning, both. I thought I'd better make an appointment before I lose my nerve!'

Katie whistled softly.

'I was afraid you'd changed your mind overnight.'

'Geoff, if you need time to think over your decision, that's fine by us. Shall we all sit down in my office?'

'No thanks, Fiona, I really would like you to put me on your books.'

'I'm so pleased.' Katie beamed.

'If it makes life easier for you, you could come up for a chat as soon after five o'clock as you can make it, any day this week,' Fiona said.

'Then let's make it today,' he said firmly.

* * *

Tim Carlisle was in a rush. He'd collected his car from the garage where he'd left it for its MOT test and, after he paid his bill, became embroiled in traffic. After he finally found a parking space near his flat, he was running late.

Tim hated being late but with a bit of luck, he could still make it on time. He loped along the pavement, crossed the road and hurried down the stone steps towards the tube trains.

He purchased a ticket, passed through the barrier and clattered down the escalator, overtaking the handful of passengers riding on it. Travelling in rush hour would have been a different matter.

On the platform he walked to the far end and within a few minutes boarded a tube train which stopped at Oxford Circus. The department store he'd suggested as suitable for a quiet afternoon tea was only a two minute walk from the station. He'd met his mother in its restaurant more than once over the few years he'd been living in London.

Tim wondered what she'd make of

him registering with a marriage bureau. She'd met his father at the local church's youth club and they were still inseparable. Would he ever, could he ever, find their kind of love and devotion?

Deep in his thoughts, it took him a while to realise the train was slowing. But they'd only just pulled out of Green Park Station. What's more, people were looking anxious as they heard the strange sounds the engine was now making. Tim checked his watch again. So near and yet so far. The train lurched to a halt and he thought the sudden silence was more worrying than the odd noises had been.

Mentally he scolded himself for not taking the bus. It was too late now.

* * *

Jenny had grasped the opportunity to do some shopping for a number of items her daughter needed now summer was in full swing.

She hoped the airline captain wouldn't mind her bringing a carrier bag along to their meeting but it seemed ridiculous not to seize this rare chance, especially as her mum had arrived to babysit earlier than anticipated.

Jenny wore a white bolero jacket over a yellow polka-dot cotton dress that suited her dark colouring. She arrived at the restaurant entrance at exactly three-thirty.

She glanced at her watch soon after arriving then walked a little further away from the entrance to wait. Within moments, a tall man wearing a sports jacket with grey trousers walked towards her, coming to a halt a couple of yards away.

This man had dark hair and though he'd glanced at her, he obviously wasn't Captain Carlisle. Jenny had walked quite a distance since leaving home at one o'clock and her feet hurt.

The high-heeled white sandals so flattering to her ankles and legs suddenly seemed like instruments of torture. She glanced at the upholstered bench nearby and went over to it, parking her bags beside her and checking her watch again.

As she looked up, she noticed the man standing alone nearby was checking his watch and frowning. Jenny turned her head away and a couple of minutes later he sat down at the other end of the bench.

She began to wonder if somehow there'd been a mix-up. Could this man be the one she was hoping to meet? If so, wouldn't he have asked her if she was waiting for someone?

How awful it would be if she plucked up courage to ask him if he was Captain Carlisle only to discover he most definitely was not! She sighed, resigning herself to watching the customers reaching the top of the escalator and moving off in all directions except hers.

At five minutes to four, the stranger sitting near her stood up and paced up and down for a while. He caught her eye as he turned back towards the bench and Jenny smiled at him.

He hesitated and walked up to her.

'Forgive me if I'm intruding, but have we both by any chance been stood up?'

She looked into the stranger's kindly, dark brown eyes and nodded.

'I certainly have, unless you happen to be called Tim and you've just dyed your hair?'

'Unfortunately, I'm not. My name is Mike and I was due to meet my sister here but she's prone to be very scatty and knowing her, she's totally forgotten she's supposed to be seeing her big brother today.' He bit his lip.

'This is an awful cheek, I know, but I'm desperate for a cup of tea and something to eat. Would you, could you, possibly consider joining me so we can save ourselves from this embarrassing situation?'

★ ★ ★

Tim, now gloomier than ever, was still sitting on the train. It was four o'clock and he was haunted by the thought of Jenny waiting for him in vain. The only positive news was that a railway official had made his way through the carriages to inform the passengers they were soon to be towed to Oxford Circus, the next tube station.

The man apologised for any inconvenience caused and some passengers grumbled at the unfortunate fellow though Tim could see no point in making a fuss.

He knew only too well how delays were part and parcel of any form of travel but he bitterly regretted having to leave Jenny stranded. There'd be no second chance, of that he was sure. And he didn't want to contemplate what Mrs Maple would say. He frowned upon realising how important her good opinion was to him.

By the time Tim was released and hurrying towards Great Salisbury Street, he was almost an hour late for his appointment. At last, on reaching the department store, he pushed through the swing doors and ran towards the upward escalator, ignoring disapproving glances from chic saleswomen and shoppers.

He climbed the moving staircase and hurtled off it close to the restaurant entrance. No sign of Jenny. But he hadn't really expected her to wait so long, had he?

Beyond the entrance, he noticed a man in a dark suit studying the busy restaurant and quickly approached him.

'Excuse me, I'm very late for an appointment and I wonder if the young lady I was due to meet has enquired about any message from me? My name's Captain Carlisle.'

'Let me check for you, sir.' The manager hastened over to the cash desk and spoke to the girl behind it.

'I'm sorry, sir. No message.'

'I see.' Tim sighed. 'Is it possible you can give me a table for one, please? This has been a very difficult day.'

The restaurant manager signalled to a waitress who led Tim to a small table well away from the entrance. He failed to notice an attractive dark-haired young woman talking animatedly to her companion while they waited for their tea to arrive.

* * *

Around four o'clock, Fiona was wondering whether Jenny and the pilot were having fun together over a delicious afternoon treat, or if one or both of them had decided this meeting was to be their first and last. It was no good trying to guess about such a delicate and intricate matter as the human heart.

Katie had recounted several instances where she'd been convinced the couple concerned were destined to be together for ever, yet the feedback afterwards proved her to be very wrong. Hopefully Tim would at least have taken trouble to dress conservatively. He had some quite flamboyant neckties which didn't worry her but it was always better to play safe at first, she'd advised him.

Geoff Wentworth arrived at about ten past five. Katie was still on the phone to one of her clients so Fiona let their neighbour in and took him through to her office.

'I still can't quite believe I'm here,' he said, sitting down.

'It's really not that terrifying a procedure!' Fiona reached for her notebook.

'I need to take a few details, such as your home address. I imagine you prefer not to have any mail connected to the bureau delivered to your office?'

'I think what you say is best,' he said. 'My secretary usually opens the mail and she's very discreet but I'd like to keep my venture to myself for the time being.'

'A good decision, Geoff. We do ask that once you have a meeting arranged between you and another of our clients, you keep that person's name confidential and instruct her to do the same.

'Sadly, some people can be a little critical of our business, something I find very unfair, when introductions can bring so much happiness. And from the feminine point of view, I think our strict procedures make the whole meeting up business far more secure than a chance encounter at a bus stop or a dance.'

Geoff was chatting to Fiona about the kind of lady he might like to meet when there was a tap at the door and Katie put her head round.

'I'm so sorry to interrupt you both,

but Fiona, could I have a quick word in private? I promise not to keep you too long.'

'I'm in no hurry,' Geoff said.

Katie closed the connecting door behind her boss and drew her further away.

'What's happened? It's not bad news, I hope.'

'I just had Tim Carlisle on the phone. He got stuck on a tube train between stations and turned up for his afternoon tea date a whole hour late.'

Fiona gasped.

'Did Jenny wait for him?'

'That's why he rang from a callbox. There was no sign of her so he checked there'd been no-one enquiring about him then had tea on his own. It was sheer bad luck and he said, though he'd been a bit pushed for time, he would've arrived by three-thirty if the train hadn't broken down.'

'Did he sound genuine?'

'I'd say so, and he's prepared to ring Jenny to explain, but he wanted your advice first, in case she's too furious to listen to his apology. He was planning to head home after ringing to consult us.'

Fiona nodded.

'OK, I'll try to speak to both of them in a while, but it's time you went home, Katie. I don't want to delay you.'

'Honestly, I'm happy to telephone Jenny while you finish talking to Geoff.'

'Well, in that case, yes please! That'd be great. I'll ring our pilot friend later, but right now, I think it's Jenny we should concentrate on, don't you?'

'I do. I'll explain what happened and ask whether Tim may ring her to apologise and, if so, whether she's agreeable to arranging another meeting.'

Warning Bells

Fiona was preparing a cheese salad when the phone in her hallway began ringing. She hurried to answer, reminding herself she needed to contact Tim Carlisle soon, though with his current run of luck, he was probably now stuck in the evening rush hour.

'It's me! And you'll never guess in a million years what's happened!'

'You sound excited, Katie. Please don't keep me in suspense.'

'I had to leave a message with Jenny's mother because she still hadn't arrived home when I rang. But no need to worry, because Jenny had rung her mum from a call box to explain she'd been delayed but was getting a lift home.'

'This gets more and more complicated.' Fiona groaned. 'How come she managed to get a lift, I wonder?'

'Her mum didn't say but I took the liberty of leaving my home number as you were still dealing with Geoff, so

Jenny rang me just now to explain what happened. Better brace yourself . . . '

Fiona listening with growing disbelief as Katie recounted the afternoon tea drama as Jenny had explained it.

'Well, what do you think of that?' Katie asked at last.

'I think it's a case of Fate taking a hand. But I winced when you said Jenny had accepted a lift from this chap, Mike.'

'I know. But she obviously went with her instincts. I should have said, he insisted on speaking to the restaurant manager and leaving his address and car registration number, to reassure Jenny he wasn't up to no good. I must say, I like the sound of him but what price our pilot now?'

'Does Jenny not want to meet Tim now? Did you ask if she'd accept his apology?'

'She doesn't want any fuss and we're not to bother him now she knows the reason for his non-appearance. She's asked if we can give her time to decide whether she wishes to receive any more introductions.'

'That sounds as though Mike has asked her out and she's accepted.'

'You got it in one, boss!'

'OK. I'm happy with that if you are. And when I speak to our lonely aviator, why don't I tell him we'll be in touch tomorrow after we've sounded out another young lady?'

'Are you thinking of the girl who works in the department store?'

'I am. The Fragrant One is next on our list of suitable introductions, but we can double check tomorrow. Thanks for all this, Katie.'

'Not at all. It's one of the many things I love about this job. The unexpected!'

★ ★ ★

Tim groaned when his telephone rang. Walking from his sitting-room to the small hallway, he decided, as he wasn't on standby, it was unlikely to be the pilots' scheduling office and highly likely he'd find himself talking either to Jenny or Mrs Maple herself. He'd spent several frustrating hours getting nowhere but if the young widow was still prepared to meet him, he was willing to give it a go.

'Good evening, Tim. Is this a good time?'

He closed his eyes as he heard the voice that haunted his thoughts far too often these days. Why, oh why, having registered with Mrs Maple's Marriage Bureau, did he have to go and fall for the proprietor herself? And a married woman at that. He took a deep breath, wondering what her husband did for a living while his wife spent her days trying to help her clients find happiness.

'Hello, Fiona. The time's fine but how come you're working such long hours?'

'Don't worry about me. It's you I'm concerned about.'

His heart bumped too madly in his chest.

'I'm more worried about that poor young woman left stranded outside the tea room as she was. I expect Katie's told you I'd like to ring and apologise?'

'She has, but please don't contact Jenny now, Tim. She understands it was circumstances beyond your control that made you so late and at least she was waiting in comfortable surroundings.'

'Poor girl. I know she was arranging for her mother to babysit, and all for nothing.'

'She did manage to go shopping first, I gather.' And find a new boyfriend into the bargain, she added silently.

'That's something, I suppose.' He hesitated. 'Dare I ask if she's prepared to arrange another meeting?'

'The thing is, Tim, Jenny has asked for some time to think about her situation. So, tomorrow, I'll speak to the next young lady we have in mind as a possible match and if she's agreeable, Katie or I will provide her contact details to you.'

Silence.

'Tim? Are you still there?'

'Erm, yeah . . . yes, I'm still here. You're doing exactly as I requested and not wasting any time. That's very good of you, Mrs . . . erm, I mean Fiona.'

'It's what we're here for.'

'I've no complaints about your service, but at this time of day, shouldn't you be sitting down with Mr Maple for your evening meal?'

★ ★ ★

Fiona felt emotionally wrung out after her conversation with Tim. She'd been concentrating upon his situation and trying to steer him into wearing more conventional socks and buy some more sedate ties, while encouraging him to remain positive.

She hadn't wanted to tell him he'd got the wrong end of the stick in assuming she was married. Why was that? Absent-mindedly she sat down at the kitchen table and began to eat her cheese salad, the radio playing quietly in the background.

Not that she could have told anyone what programme she was listening to. No, her head was in the clouds, as her father would have told her in no uncertain terms.

On the other hand, mightn't she be getting too involved with her clients? Katie had passed on that warning to Fiona, just as Great-aunt Millie had passed it to her.

That's why Fiona had stammered out some rubbish about this fictitious husband not being around. Well, that much was the truth anyway.

Timothy Carlisle had sounded rather depressed, poor man. Fiona gave herself a mental shake-up. Why on earth hadn't she told Tim the absolute truth, not fudged around it?

Yet, she argued to herself, that shouldn't be an issue. He was one of her clients and she had her professional integrity to consider.

But because she was beginning to see him as a friend and not merely a client, warning bells were ringing in her head, and to maintain the married status which he believed she held, seemed to be the right option, also the safest.

The man was looking for a wife and it was no good her mooning over him, even if he was proving something of a challenge for the bureau. She decided to ask Katie to ring Captain Carlisle once they had the go ahead from their saleslady client.

Pleased with her decision, Fiona picked up a teaspoon to eat her carton of yoghurt, totally forgetting she hadn't yet taken the lid off.

* * *

The following Saturday Timothy Carlisle was nursing a cup of tea while waiting in a café close to the big store where his next prospective wife worked in the perfume department.

He disliked referring to someone as a possible match or a candidate, but then, there was nothing he particularly liked about the process anyway. Except for Mrs Maple. She was so easy to talk to. Well, Katie was fine, too, but on the few occasions he'd been face to face with

Fiona, he remembered how she looked at him as if she really cared about his future happiness.

It occurred to him that probably every male client on her database held the same opinion and that it meant nothing other than she was a caring, efficient professional who enjoyed her work.

He counted in his head how many young women he'd now met. After Rosemary, who quite frankly had terrified him, there'd been two in fairly swift succession. One had made him feel as though he was being interrogated by the Secret Service and the other had wanted to drag him off to look at an exhibition of modern art.

He'd done his best to be polite, but unable to warm to the paintings, he'd been mightily relieved when the young lady in question had looked at her watch and declared she needed to catch her train and, no, she didn't need walking to the station, thank you.

Now he was due to meet Belinda who worked in another of London's big department stores, but thankfully she'd suggested they met in this café where she would look for him after she finished work.

They'd both agreed to play it by ear after chatting for a while, though Tim felt it would only be gentlemanly to take Belinda out for an early Saturday evening meal, though only if they could manage to keep a conversation going without awful silences and awkward moments.

He knew his date had light brown hair which she wore in a chignon for work and he imagined she'd be wearing a summery kind of dress as the temperature had risen, making the days much warmer since the beginning of the month, which had felt more like January than June.

The café door opened twice more as he waited, but only to admit a man, then an elderly couple. Tim checked his watch and realised Belinda was already ten minutes late. Well, at least he wasn't the culprit this time.

He sipped his tea, grimaced on realising he'd let it go cold, then picked up an evening newspaper left on a nearby chair and turned to the sports section.

Next time the doorbell clanged, Tim looked up, saw a young woman entering, looked away at once then looked back, his throat drying as he told himself not to leap to his feet and accost the wrong girl!

Because this one didn't seem to fit the description given him by Katie. But he rose from his chair, almost knocking it over in his haste, as the newcomer caught his eye, smiled confidently and headed straight for him.

★ ★ ★

Fiona lay curled up on the settee half-watching an episode of 'Dr Who'. But even the exuberant Tom Baker wearing his long stripy scarf while skirmishing with the Daleks couldn't keep her mind from wandering. Dangerously, at that.

She'd spoken to her parents earlier that evening and she knew her mother especially was concerned about her daughter's social life, or rather the lack of it.

Although she and Katie occasionally went to a cinema after work, you couldn't exactly describe that as a social event. They'd both enjoyed another meal with Geoff Wentworth recently, as they knew he'd been a little crushed when the first match they found for him decided he wasn't really her type.

'Honestly,' Katie had said after Geoff left their office, having reported this, 'some people are so impatient. She could at least have agreed to meet him one more time.'

'I'm not so sure about that,' Fiona had argued. 'If a person instantly feels something's not right, surely it would be pointless — even cruel — to agree to a second date?'

Fiona's mum didn't think that kind of socialising was a very good idea.

'You shouldn't be letting the day job take over your leisure time as well,' she'd insisted. 'Why don't you come and visit us one weekend, sweetheart? Get out from the city and enjoy some home cooking.

'Your dad and I would come to London but you know what he's like about the garden this time of year.'

'Oh, I do,' Fiona had agreed. 'I'll come and see you soon, Mum, but I need to feel on top of everything here before I take a couple of days off.

'Travelling on a Friday evening is never fun, so when I can, I'll arrange to leave Katie in charge and get a Friday morning train home and maybe come back to London on the Monday morning.'

Her mum had liked that idea but having put down the phone, Fiona knew in her heart she didn't really fancy leaving London just yet.

But she accepted the need to get out more. Everyone kept saying so. At least, Katie and Geoff were, though he was a fine one to talk! Still, he'd taken the plunge and hopefully the nice young woman who worked for the Civil Service and who hated parties and dances might find a kindred soul in Geoff.

For some reason, she thought of her former boyfriend and how he'd reacted when she told him she felt they had no future together. Daniel hadn't been exactly heartbroken and now it seemed to her he'd enjoyed being part of a couple rather than thinking of her as someone he might want to spend the rest of his life with. Fiona was certain many of her clients held the same view.

A shiver ran down her spine as she realised how easy it would have been to stay in the comfortable place she'd existed in, and keep going out with Daniel.

The news of her great-aunt's bequest arrived after she'd made the break and from her position now, she knew she would still have said goodbye to Daniel and seized this strange new opportunity with both hands.

On the TV screen, The Doctor and his plucky assistant had seen off the latest invasion of aliens and the credits were rolling. But in Fiona's mind's eye, it was Timothy Carlisle's face she saw.

And she couldn't help wondering

whether he was at that moment seated opposite the Fragrant One, gazing into her sparkling eyes and deciding he'd finally met a girl he wanted to see again.

She found that thought surprisingly painful.

* * *

Tim was escorting Belinda to a French restaurant not far from the café. She'd barely stopped talking since she first greeted him and, though a little irritating, it was comforting not having to find topics to talk about.

He'd looked twice at her when she walked into the café because she was wearing her hair loose around her shoulders and her dress style was more outgoing than Katie had described.

The shocking pink long-line jacket worn unbuttoned over a pair of matching hot pants probably didn't belong to someone who might object to a chap wearing a brightly coloured necktie. She wore pink suede shoes with ankle straps and wedge heels and the total effect was stunning.

However, he'd taken Mrs Maple's advice to heart and tonight even super-critical Rosemary Blake would surely not have been able to find fault with his appearance.

As they turned off Oxford Street and walked down a side street, Tim was wondering, while Belinda chattered about the perfume she'd sold that day, whether he should have rung to book a table. But it was too late now and to be fair, they had decided in their preliminary phone call only to go for a meal if they seemed to be getting on well together.

On arriving at the restaurant, he realised there'd be no trouble finding a table and soon the two of them were sitting opposite one another, menus in hand.

'What do you recommend?' Belinda asked, looking up at him. Was she really fluttering her eyelashes?

'Honestly, everything's always very good so please choose what you like.'

'I adore truffles but what are they doing under the starters?'

Ah, is she teasing me or is she mistaking the fungi for the chocolate and rum sweetie that everyone's aunt makes at Christmas? He didn't know. Decided to call her bluff.

'I have no idea,' he said. 'Must be new to the menu since my last visit.' He smiled at her, thinking she really did have the most beautiful brown eyes.

Her lips were twitching.

'I was expecting a lecture, but you surprised me, Tim. Is it all right to call you Tim?'

'Of course, Belinda. Or do you prefer another version of your name?'

'Belinda's fine, or Bel if you wish. And I'm not into underground fungi so I think I'd like the soup, please.'

He grinned.

'I'll go for that, too. And I can recommend their fish of the day or the boeuf bourguignon.'

'I'd like the beef, I think.'

'Me too.' Tim sat back as the wine waiter arrived, bearing a bottle of Beaujolais.

'This wine's very mellow and it'll go well with the meat.'

Left alone again, Tim raised his glass to Belinda.

'Your good health.'

She echoed the toast.

'You're much posher than me, Tim.' She sniffed her wine then took a sip.

'Posher? Goodness, I don't think so. My dad's a farmer up north but he's not one of the landed gentry, thank goodness. I don't think I could've coped with having to follow in his footsteps and run a large estate.'

'But you're a pilot. All pilots are posh.'

He burst out laughing.

'Ah, I'm sorry, Belinda, but we really aren't superior beings, you know. My dad tells his friends I'm a glorified bus driver!'

She chuckled.

'Cheeky! I'd tell him off if I was you.'

'You speak beautifully,' Tim said. 'I bet your customers think you're posh.' He sipped his wine then broke open the warm bread roll that had just arrived.

The evening was becoming very enjoyable.

He even felt guilty for wishing Belinda wouldn't turn up so he could head for home, picking up a takeaway from the place near his flat.

'I speak differently when I'm with my folks,' she said.

He sat back open-mouthed as she imitated Eliza Doolittle before Professor Higgins took charge of her elocution.

'Strike a light! You should see the expression on your boat race.' She ended with a peal of laughter.

'What's my boat race?' Light dawned. 'Ah, you mean my face. You can't expect a boy from oop north to understand your rhyming slang, you know.'

They chatted and laughed their way through the soup, then the delicious beef stew, and lingered over the crème caramel they'd each chosen. Neither mentioned the marriage bureau or their expectations and Tim was feeling far more positive than he'd felt in quite some while.

Belinda asked him about the routes he flew and he spoke of his favourite cities and the way he and his crews needed to become accustomed to living out of a suitcase.

In her turn, she told him about the huge number of ingredients and the delicate balance between perfume oil and alcohol necessary to create a fabulous scent. After asking him to lean towards her, she told him what kind of aftershave he was wearing.

'I'm impressed,' he said.

'I help lots of women choose aftershave for their menfolk but mostly I stand behind a counter, selling scent to men wanting to find a gift for their wives or girlfriends.

'We consultants are advised how to do our hair and of course we learn make up skills so we can not only look glamorous in the store, but know how to advise our customers.' She smiled. 'By mid-afternoon, all we're wishing is that we could take off our shoes!'

'You know,' he said, 'in some ways

that's similar to being an air stewardess. The having to look glamorous bit,
however they might be feeling. You must
smile and greet people a lot in the store.'

'Part of the job.' Belinda put down
her dessert spoon. 'You've just got me
thinking again. I've always wished I was
confident enough to apply to be an air
stewardess.'

He stared back at her. What was this?
She certainly didn't sound like someone
who was looking for a serious personal
relationship in her life.

'Oh, dear,' she said, before he could
respond. 'Please don't think this is anything to do with you being an airline
pilot, but becoming an air stewardess has always been a dream job to me
though I've never admitted it to anyone
before. Of course, I have as much chance
of it happening as I have of going over
Niagara Falls in a barrel!'

He smiled.

'You should never ignore a dream like
that, Belinda. I dreamed of learning to
fly when I was a little boy and I made it

happen. I know you're over twenty-one which airline stewardesses have to be, so why haven't you applied to an airline by now?' Tim thought she was looking a little shamefaced.

'How are you on paperwork? You know you'd have to sell drinks and add up bar accounts at the end of a flight?'

She leaned towards him, hands clasped beneath her chin.

'I did well in my exams, especially Maths, but I didn't want to go on studying. And my parents aren't that well off so I wanted to begin earning. But having worked at the store for so long, I'm afraid of applying for something new and being rejected.

'All I've done since leaving school is retail. I began as a junior in a clothing department, then two years ago I applied to work in perfumery. I enjoy it, but I feel there's something missing from my life. That's really why I contacted Mrs Maple. And now I've met you and look what a mess I'm making of it!'

'Not at all,' he reassured her. 'It's just

as well you've spoken so honestly to me so we both know where we stand.'

'I imagine there's no way you'd want to see me again.' She avoided looking at him.

'Nonsense! I enjoy your company very much but I think for the time being we both need to put thoughts of marriage out of our minds, don't you?'

He hesitated, wondering how best to handle this situation, but feeling oddly relieved by Belinda's blurted out wish. He could help her achieve this, he knew he could. Meanwhile, the pair of them must consider the marriage bureau's point of view and surely it wouldn't hurt to arrange another meeting?

'If you'll allow me,' he said, 'I'll help you with your application for training as an air stewardess and if you're successful, you'll have a lot of things to think about and marriage shouldn't be one of them. I'm sure that'll happen for you some time in the future but meanwhile I hope we can become friends. How does that sound?'

Unexpected Romance

Tim arrived home having seen Belinda to her train station and kissed her cheek before waving goodbye. He'd written down the addresses of two airlines including the one for which he flew, telling her she should start with these, because they recruited all year round. He also promised that if she received an application form from either or both of them, he'd help her complete it. She'd seemed thrilled and not at all disappointed by not seeing him again for at least a week.

This, he told himself, meant that, like him, Belinda felt nothing stronger than friendship.

She'd been thrilled to find he considered her a suitable applicant for cabin crew, telling him she must begin watching her weight, in the remote possibility that she might gain an interview. He told her that was a sensible thing to do anyway, but that she looked absolutely fine to him.

The evening had been an eye-opener to Tim. After Belinda revealed her dream, his feeling of relief surprised him. Marriage wasn't an option for the majority of air stewardesses though he believed some airlines were beginning to alter their rules. But if Belinda was truly serious about applying, she'd go on a training course before taking examinations to prove she knew her stuff.

He understood only too well how demanding a job in aviation could be and though many airline personnel went on dates with others in the same business, conflicting schedules were always an issue.

He decided the best thing to do was wait until he saw Belinda again and could ask her how she planned to deal with Mrs Maple's procedures. She could, he supposed, request her registration to be kept on hold while she sorted out her career prospects. But in his case, he'd made no secret of how much loneliness was part of his way of life and he was well aware how revealing this might not have been such a good idea.

He couldn't keep stalling Mrs Maple and her assistant, that was for sure. But his track record as a candidate wasn't looking good.

★ ★ ★

Next morning, Tim rang the bureau, spoke to Katie and informed her that he and Belinda were planning another meeting but his schedule didn't allow this to happen yet.

He'd be in touch regarding progress but meanwhile he hoped they'd bear with him. After he rang off, Katie went in to confer with Fiona, who'd just been speaking to a new client.

'The dashing captain and the fragrant Belinda seem to have hit it off well,' she announced.

Fiona experienced a pang of something unexpected. She'd almost felt panicked by hearing this but that was just plain stupid, surely?

'Are you all right?' Katie was looking concerned. 'You haven't got much colour in your cheeks this morning.'

'I'm fine, thanks. Just a little under the weather — you know.'

Katie nodded in sympathy.

'Poor you. Hope it passes soon. But that's good news from Tim Carlisle, don't you think?'

'Yes, I do. Yes, it's very good news.' Fiona forced a smile. 'Maybe we're finally getting somewhere.'

'He's promised to keep us informed but he'll be out of the country for a while, so probably won't be able to meet up with Belinda until at least next week. I'll write a note in both their files then I'll make us both a cuppa. Did you have breakfast?'

'You're like a mother hen with a chick!' Fiona chuckled. 'I skipped it this morning.'

'Then tea and digestive biscuits will be coming your way very soon and that's a promise.' Katie made her exit.

Fiona sat staring into the distance.

She really ought to do what everyone kept saying she should do. Katie had researched a film society and taken note of the phone number. Too much brooding about what she couldn't have while on her own in the flat each evening was no way to make the most of her new life in London.

Realising Katie was busy with tea-making, when the telephone rang, Fiona answered it at once.

'Mrs Maple's Marriage Bureau. Fiona Maple speaking.'

'Just the lady!'

She recognised the voice immediately.

'Good morning, Geoff. How are things?'

He didn't reply for a few moments.

'Actually, I'm in a bit of a quandary and I wondered whether you were free tonight. I'd like to buy you dinner and bend your ear if you can possibly bear it.'

He was a nice man and if he had something worrying him, trying to help Geoff would be better than brooding over her own ridiculous daydreams.

'I'm happy to help if I can,' she said. 'Just tell me what time you'll be ready and I'll see you downstairs after work.'

Katie's reaction to knowing her boss was spending the evening with Geoff was strangely prickly.

'I hope he's not going to be a nuisance.' She was hovering in Fiona's doorway after delivering the promised tea and biscuits.

'Why do you say that? He's a perfectly pleasant man who probably wants a sympathetic ear. He knows you have your folks to go back to, whereas I'm on my own.'

'Oh, I'm not put out because I'm not invited. I'm just concerned he might be getting a little too fond of you.'

'Geoff? Too fond of me?' Fiona laughed out loud. 'I don't think so for one minute, but if it makes you feel any better, I think of him as a client who's become a mate.

'It'd give me the greatest of pleasure to hear he's fallen in love with the lady he's been seeing. But he's so shy and retiring, maybe he wants a bit of advice. Come to think of it, he'd be better off asking you, Katie, seeing as how you're the one who's married!'

★ ★ ★

Over spaghetti bolognese and a cheeky carafe of rosé in the Italian restaurant, Geoff lost no time in explaining his predicament.

'It's Jane,' he said. 'My secretary.'

'Oh dear, I hope she's not ill? Katie has the number of an excellent agency if you're stuck.'

'No, no — she's in the pink. But I confided in her recently that I was going out with someone and since then, things have changed between us.'

'Between you and Jane? But you've been seeing Helen and getting on well. Or have I got my wires crossed?'

'Helen's a lovely lady and I've been thinking how well we get on. Yet we're more like brother and sister, to be honest.' He fixed his gaze on a spot somewhere

179

above Fiona's dark head. 'There's no spark between us, if you know what I mean.'

Fiona remained silent while the waiter topped up their glasses. She smiled her thanks and he flashed his dark eyes at her as he moved away.

'Well, you certainly have a fan there,' Geoff said. 'Can't help but agree with him. I often wonder why no-one has snapped you up, Fiona.'

'We're here to talk about you,' she said. 'Don't change the subject. I want to hear about you and Jane.'

'She was in my office, taking dictation, when Helen rang me to say she might be a few minutes late getting away from work that evening. After I put down the phone, I could see Jane looking curious so I confessed I'd been seeing a young lady for some few weeks.

'Jane looked so shocked, then so distraught, I found myself getting up from my chair and going around the desk to comfort her.' He gulped and looked embarrassed.

'It's all right, Geoff. I think I'm getting the picture. It sounds to me as though your secretary has been carrying a torch for you for a while now but not known what to do about it. Then you suddenly tell her you have a lady friend and it dawns on her that she's missed her chance. Is that about it?'

'Well, yes, except she hasn't missed her chance, has she?'

Fiona leaned forward, hands clasped in front of her.

'Obviously not. I can tell from your face.'

'I can only say, I must have been sleepwalking. Jane has worked for me for five years now.'

'Sometimes these things take time. But did you meet Helen that evening as planned? I haven't heard anything from her since you started seeing one another.'

'Oh yes, I met her. I wouldn't let anyone down unless something very unusual occurred.'

'And how did Jane feel about that?'

Fiona watched Geoff's cheeks turn a

delicate shade of pink.

'We, um, actually kissed for the first time after she told me she couldn't bear the thought of me being in love with someone else. Luckily for me, light dawned and I told her I wasn't in love with anyone else and as soon as the words left my mouth, I knew Jane was the woman I wanted. That's when I kissed her.'

'And she kissed you back?'

'Um, yes. Gosh, yes, she did!'

'And what advice do you need? You seem to be doing very well on your own account.' She grinned at him. 'I imagine you'd like me to speak to Helen?'

'Only if you think that's a good idea. Asking you to tell her seems so cowardly, yet I can't bear the thought of hurting her.'

The waiter was back, shooting glances at Fiona while clearing their plates. He returned with the dessert menu and Geoff asked for a few more minutes.

'Please, Fiona, what do you think is best?' Geoff still looked anxious.

'The tiramisu sounds wonderful!' Fiona

chuckled. 'I'm teasing you. If you want my honest opinion, from what you've told me, my guess is Helen also recognises that though you two get on well, it's never going to be a great romance.

'And though you told me when you registered that you were looking for a companionable relationship, now you've set the sparks flying between you and Jane, you know Helen and you can't go on meeting.'

His eyes sparkled.

'You're absolutely right. Helen deserves to hear the truth from me but I do hope you can find her ideal man.'

'We'll try our best.'

'Let's order our desserts. Tiramisu for us both, I think. And I can't thank you enough.'

'But we didn't find you the right person! You've done that for yourself, Geoffrey Wentworth.'

'Maybe. But if weren't for you and Katie, I'd never have plucked up courage to register and to go out with Helen in the first place. My doing so has caused

Jane to wake up and . . . '

Fiona reached out to pat his hand.

'As long as there's a happy ending, that's all that matters.'

Next morning, Fiona told Katie she had some unexpected news. She explained about Geoff's surprise confession and her assistant agreed with what Fiona thought was the most professional way to deal with the situation. Geoff would write to Helen, who he'd been out with four times, and explain in his own words why he thought they shouldn't go on meeting. Fiona would allow time for the letter to arrive before ringing their client to make sure she was all right.

'If she'd like to come here and talk things through, I'll fit in with her, whatever time it is,' Fiona said.

'I'm really pleased for Geoff, but I hope Helen won't be too upset. She's a lovely woman.' Katie tapped her pen against her teeth. 'I also hope this won't put her off the agency. Business has picked up a lot over the summer but it'd be a shame to lose two clients at once.'

'She strikes me as down-to-earth,' Fiona said, 'and, who knows, she might even be relieved at the thought of meeting someone new. That lovely driving instructor I saw the other day is about her age and we haven't arranged any introductions for him yet.'

'Fingers crossed Helen stays with us, then.'

'By the way, Geoff insists he doesn't want his fee back,' Fiona said. 'He says it's entirely his fault that he doesn't want to go ahead with any more contacts and he wouldn't expect a refund. What do you think?'

'I think that's fair. We've done some work on his behalf and would have gone on doing so. No need for us to feel guilty about hanging on to his fee, in my opinion.'

'So, we no longer have to think about Geoff's romantic life and now our dashing pilot might have found true love with the Fragrant One, who knows?' Fiona tried to speak lightly but wished she didn't feel so weighed down.

'He won't be back in London for a while yet anyway. I think it's time for me to go right through the filing cabinet and make sure we haven't been lagging behind in any way.'

Katie gave her a shrewd look.

'OK. I'll type a couple of welcome letters first.' She glanced at her open diary. 'You're interviewing that titled lady this morning. I'm always amazed when these former debs contact us. You'd think they'd have met scores of eligible males at parties and dances, wouldn't you?'

'It's a long time since the whole debutante ritual was the thing for posh young ladies. I read all about it in one of Millie's books. No more girls were presented to the Queen and Prince Philip after 1958 and although Queen Charlotte's Birthday Ball still takes place each year, they say it's unlikely to continue.'

Katie nodded.

'Life has changed dramatically, what with the Swinging Sixties and other things your great-aunt must have disapproved of! She was never stiff and starchy but Millie had very strict rules that were designed for everyone's welfare. I think she knew you'd want to continue in the same way, when it came to security and confidentiality.'

'Thanks, Katie. But it's you who has taught me all I know. Thank goodness you were happy to stay on and work with me.'

'Nonsense! I knew you'd be fine. You're a more experienced secretary than me, for one thing.'

'It's lucky we both like the same office systems but I couldn't have done without you boosting my confidence when it came to interviewing the clients.'

Katie smiled.

'You were thrown in at the deep end and you're doing a brilliant job.' She hesitated. 'Before we get to work, could I check out some dates for my summer hols?'

'Of course. I doubt I'll be taking any but I'd like to visit my parents soon and make it a long weekend if that's all right with you.'

'I expect they're longing for you to visit,' Katie said. 'I wouldn't normally ask for leave in August but my husband is due back in the first week of the month.'

'I'm so pleased for you. You must take a fortnight.'

'Thank you. I'll confirm the exact dates as soon as he lets me know. I think he wants to whisk me away to a small hotel somewhere near Edinburgh. He went there for a friend's wedding some years ago and thinks it's time I visited his homeland.'

'Lucky you!' Fiona felt wistful. 'I'd love to see Edinburgh.'

'Well, you have time. Forgive me for asking, but does your old boyfriend ever get in touch? Feel free to tell me off if I'm being too nosy!'

'Not at all. Daniel obviously didn't take long to forget me. Mum heard through the grapevine that he asked one of my friends to go with him and they've been seeing each other ever since.'

'Does that bother you?'

'Not in the least. I'm pleased for him and I know what Geoff means when he talks about there being no spark between him and Helen. I believe there's such a thing as love at first sight, but I also believe that sometimes it can take quite a while for that elusive spark to flare.'

Hope on the Horizon

Captain Tim Carlisle walked across the richly carpeted foyer of his New York hotel, wondering what Fiona Maple was doing at that moment. How silly was that?

Calculating the time between where he was and where she was, Mrs Maple was probably making supper for her husband. Or perhaps lucky Mr Maple was cooking for his lovely wife? Trying to ignore a jealous pang, he almost walked past a tall man leaving the lift Tim was about to enter.

'Hey! If it's not young Carlisle! We must stop meeting like this.'

Tim felt his grin almost split his face as he shook the older man's hand.

'It's a pleasure to bump into you again, Gus. Can't keep away from the old company's favourite hotel then?'

'I asked to stay here and the answer was yes. Aviation's a small world in some ways.'

'Are you in a hurry or do you have

time for a drink?'

'Actually, I was wondering whether to order tea in the lounge or go out and find somewhere not too noisy.'

'Then let's try the latter option.'

'As long as I'm not taking you away from your crew?'

'Not at all. We're all meeting up for dinner together later. Tomorrow we have an early alarm call then it's off to the airport and back home.'

As he fell into step with the older man, Tim knew Gus was bound to ask whether he'd taken his former mentor's advice regarding his personal life and if so, how he was getting on. But it was great to meet up with the man he so respected and to whom he had cause to be grateful.

'I discovered a little place when I was here last,' Tim said. 'It's just round the corner from the hotel.'

'Sounds good to me. Still enjoying your flying?'

'Can't complain. But what are you doing in the Big Apple, Gus, if it's not too impertinent a question?'

'I'm speaking at a conference tomorrow. Goodness knows why anyone would invite me, but my wife's delighted because she's here, too. Out shopping at this moment with an old college friend who married an American and settled in New York years ago.'

Tim nodded.

'No prizes for guessing why you're in demand as a speaker. You must have taught countless men and women to fly. And with all that RAF action behind you — the Americans won't know what's hit them!'

'You're very kind.'

'And you must be pleased to have your wife with you too.'

'Yes, indeed. I'm very fortunate to have remarried and still be able to enjoy a little jaunt. We're staying on for a few more nights to do some sightseeing.'

Tim knew Gus had lost his first wife before he met him on his training course, but that he'd found happiness with a lady who had also been widowed. He gestured to a café just ahead of them, where people were relaxing at tables outside.

'This is it. Inside or outside?'

'I'm fine outside under a sun umbrella. And you can do with all the fresh air you can get.'

Tim grinned.

'We get used to being cooped up inside a giant sardine can, don't we?' He pulled out a chair for his friend.

Gus gave him a playful punch on the arm.

'Now you're making me feel old!'

'You? Never!' Tim sat down opposite and gave their order to the waiter who appeared moments later. 'I've been wondering whether you took my advice.'

'And what advice would that be?' Tim pretended to look puzzled.

'Come off it, Carlisle! Did you sign on with Mrs M's outfit?'

'I did.'

'And? You're stuck with me now so better come clean!'

'I've registered, yes. And I must say thank you for the recommendation.

The organisation seems to run very effi-
ciently.'

'Is that lovable old dear still running
the show? Though come to think of it, I
imagine she must be retired by now.'

Tim felt puzzled.

'I'm not sure who you mean. There's
certainly no older lady working there
now.'

Gus sat back.

'Ah, then Mrs Maple, having brought
as many couples together as I've taught
whippersnappers to fly an aeroplane, must
have hung up her matchmaking gloves.'

Tim slid one finger round the inside
of his collar.

'Well, the Mrs Maple who interviewed
me is in her early twenties, I guess, and
she . . . well, she's a very attractive young
woman.'

Gus stared at him but didn't have time
to speak as the tea tray things were being
unloaded on the table.

'Right,' he said after the waiter left.
'My Mrs Maple had to be at least eighty.
I don't recall her secretary's name but

she was very young. Maybe twenty or twenty-one if my memory's not playing tricks.'

'Can you remember her name?' Tim asked.

'Let me think . . . was it Kathy? No, she was called Katie.'

Tim's heart was beating far too quickly for an off-duty airline pilot accustomed to dealing with all kinds of emergencies in the flight simulator where he'd spent many a happy or challenging hour with Gus.

He wasn't sure what was going on here, but Fiona had definitely not corrected him when he addressed her as Mrs Maple when they first met.

She'd told him she preferred to use her first name when she got to know a client and she in turn had called him Tim, though sometimes, jokingly, she'd address him as Captain.

His head was whirling with what-ifs but he was currently on a different continent from the person who could solve this mystery.

Gus was eager to know how many young women Tim had met so far and was amused to hear about the glamorous but steely Rosemary, who Tim thought must have finished her modelling career by then. Letting all his experiences out, including his anxious hour stuck in the tube train between stations, and how his last prospect turned out to be dreaming of her own airline career, was a great relief.

'Well, well,' Gus said while they waited to settle the bill, 'will you accept any more introductions, or will you wait and see how this latest young lady gets on with her applications?'

'I think Belinda and I will stay in touch. I've never had a female friend who isn't also working in aviation before — well, not since my student days.'

'If she's accepted for stewardess training, you still won't!' Gus grinned. 'Forgive me, but when you were speaking about this Fiona who you reckon is running the business now, your face gave you away, old chap. I think she's the one you've fallen for, only you've somehow got your knickers in a twist and decided she's the Mrs Maple on the letterheading. Am I right?'

★ ★ ★

Contrary to how Tim imagined Fiona to be spending her evening, while he drank tea with his old friend in New York, she was sitting in an art house cinema in London's Maida Vale, trying to understand the plot of the black and white film she was watching.

Even though English subtitles accompanied the action, she still hadn't a clue as to what was going on.

The woman who'd welcomed her on arrival in the foyer, and others in the group, appeared to be enjoying the drama, so Fiona decided there must be something wrong with her. Maybe her IQ wasn't high enough? It was depressing.

And what's more, with Katie counting down the days until her husband returned and Geoff Wentworth walking

197

around with an irritatingly dreamy smile on his chops, she was beginning to think she was in the wrong business.

Why couldn't she fall in love? Was she incapable of learning how? All she could do was keep thinking of a certain face, belonging to a certain man who was off limits. No way could a matchmaker make advances to one of her clients!

However, seeing Geoff and his secretary Jane together, looking so happy, couldn't fail to make her feel pleased for the couple.

The summer was rolling along very delightfully, the perfect backdrop for young lovers and for not so young ones. But Fiona felt wistful as she mused how, while others were singing songs of love, they certainly weren't aimed at her.

Eventually, to her relief, the film drew to a close. There had been more than one person killed after opening their front door to a complete stranger, but the murderer (who appeared to have no particular motive but maybe Fiona's French wasn't up to the mark) having confessed, was led away to the cells.

That left the detective hero and the pretty girl who'd escaped becoming the next victim, to walk into the sunset together. Everyone clapped and a man seated behind Fiona tapped her on the shoulder and asked if she was staying for coffee.

As the group filed into the room put aside for them, Fiona took heart when she heard a couple of women saying they hadn't a clue what all that was about. So, when Katie and Geoff cross-examined her next day, she could say she wasn't the only one left puzzled by the plotline. And it seemed she now had an admirer . . .

★ ★ ★

Tim and his crew completed the formalities next morning at the airport. He enjoyed flying with this particular crew who gelled together well and he had a couple of free days to look forward to, followed by a spell on stand-by when he had to stay close to his phone, in case someone rang in sick.

His car was waiting where he'd left it and he was soon driving home. Crunch time! He wasn't exactly sure how to handle this very personal matter, but now he'd accepted his feelings and Gus had summed up the situation with his usual shrewdness, Tim knew he must discover whether Fiona was single. Or not. But, even if she was, she might already have a boyfriend.

While waiting for traffic lights to change, he had an idea.

He didn't want to embarrass Fiona so the obvious thing to do was to confide in her assistant. He'd noticed that Katie wore a wedding ring. Why hadn't he ever properly taken on board that Fiona didn't?

His lane of traffic was moving again. Soon he'd be parking, grabbing his overnight bag and briefcase and letting himself into his flat. That was the bit he disliked most. Walking into an empty apartment. Silly really, as women were holding down all kinds of jobs and even when they married, continued to do so why should he expect any wife of his to be sitting at home waiting for him to return from flying around the globe?

He realised he was an old-fashioned kind of chap, yet he'd have no objection to his fiancée or wife following her own career. Indeed, it would be wonderful to have someone to cook supper for if he was the one at home while she was at work. Someone who he knew longed to see him again, just as he longed to see her.

With his erratic flying schedule, he couldn't even keep a dog. That pleasure must be put on hold until he was more settled. But would that day ever come? He loved flying and hoped to continue with his career, preferably with the right woman sharing his life.

His thoughts returned to Fiona. Then he remembered Belinda. He'd promised to help her and of course he'd do so. He knew each of them was keen to remain friends. But no more arranged meetings. Not while he longed to take the bureau's boss in his arms!

201

Once back in his flat, he found he had two messages on his answering machine. One was from Belinda, saying she'd received an application form from one of the airlines he suggested. She sounded excited and wondered if they could meet as soon as possible.

He smiled to himself. This was a girl who'd used her initiative and though she'd originally decided a husband was the way forward, fate had thrown Tim Carlisle in her path and it looked as though she might be taking an unexpected direction.

The second message was from Katie, calling from Mrs Maple's Marriage Bureau. She hoped he'd had a good trip and wondered whether he could drop by and discuss where they went from here. She mentioned Belinda had been in touch, asking for her registration to be kept on hold for a while, because something else was taking her attention. Katie said that was fine, but meanwhile, would Tim like to meet some other young lady?

He played both messages back one

more time. Belinda didn't have an answering machine but he could wait until that evening and speak to her after she returned from the store.

As soon as he was ready, he'd walk to Marble Arch. He could do with the exercise but he also needed to see Katie, so it might mean a wait if she happened to be with another client. What he'd do if that was the case and Fiona offered to see him, he'd no idea. He'd have to wing it. Tim chuckled at his own joke.

* * *

Fiona heard Katie go to the door and let someone in. She heard the sound of a male voice but Katie was obviously taking whoever it was straight into her office. That was fine. Fiona was waiting for a client she was particularly fond of, a much older lady who hoped to meet a gentleman of around sixty-five years of age, as the lady herself was aged sixty-three.

Fiona had two possibilities in mind,

each of them a widower, and she thought her lady client would get on with either, as all of them longed to meet someone they could go on holiday with and share new experiences before it was too late.

Fiona admired these older clients for taking matters in their own hands, and not only because of the income generated. She genuinely liked helping people and was trying not to let her own yearnings take over her common sense.

When the doorbell rang again, she hurried to let her client in and settled her in the comfortable chair facing Mrs Maple's beautiful antique desk.

Fiona hurried off to make tea, wondering whether to tap on Katie's door to see if she and whoever else was in there also fancied a cuppa, then decided against it. Having made two cups of best Yorkshire tea, apparently her great-aunt's favourite brew, Fiona listened, jotted down notes, and realised, to her delight, that one of the two elderly gentlemen on her books, on paper anyway, promised to be the perfect match for the lady sitting opposite. She thought she heard sounds of movement from Katie and her visitor but concentrated upon her client.

She was still talking to her when she realised it was gone five o'clock but she didn't try to rush the interview she was conducting. People's hopes and fears were important and in a funny kind of way, she almost felt as though her great-aunt was standing at her shoulder, giving her blessing.

A Shocking Scene

After seeing her cheerful client out of the office, Fiona went to find Katie but realised she must already have left. That was a little odd, as normally, each of them managed to communicate with the other, by a discreet tap on the door and a quick 'Goodbye' or 'I'm off now', mouthed round it if the other was still interviewing.

Katie must have thought it best not to interrupt, knowing Fiona's client appreciated her full attention. No problem. Fiona gazed out at the evening sunshine bathing everything in a gentle glow. She'd tidied away her paperwork and it seemed sensible to lock up the office and walk to the park.

Geoff was leaving, too, as she headed down the stairs.

'Hello, there,' he called. 'I'm being abandoned this evening. Jane's off out to her mum's. One of those Tupperware parties, I think she said.'

'Aha!' Fiona gave him a wicked grin. 'Stocking up her bottom drawer, is she, Geoff?'

'Gosh, I hope so,' he said. 'I still can't believe how lucky we are, Fiona. Now, where are you off to, if I may make so bold?'

'I was heading for the park, actually. It's such a lovely evening.'

'It certainly is. Mind if I join you for a stroll? It seems a shame to rush off for my train while the sun's still shining.'

'I'd enjoy your company. And I promise not to ask you when you plan on proposing!'

They began walking down the street towards the busy junction at the end. Traffic was streaming by and Fiona was listening to Geoff saying how he planned to buy an engagement ring for Jane, having established her favourite gemstone when gazing into various jewellers' windows.

'I see no reason for hanging about,' he said as they stood waiting at the kerbside.

'I don't blame you,' Fiona said, glancing over at the window of the small café nearby. At once she froze. She could see not one but two familiar faces.

This café wasn't one the locals used as it was mostly patronised by tourists, yet here was Katie — with Tim Carlisle next to her. The pair were seated on stools at the counter facing on to the pavement, tall milkshake glasses in front of them and deep in conversation.

Seeing this, Fiona felt her heart react in a way that made her gasp with the sheer shock of seeing the little tableau. She turned her back on the scene and swayed slightly, trying to make sense of what was going on.

'Lights have changed!' Geoff gently took her elbow and guided her across. To her horror, she couldn't stop herself trembling and when they reached the other pavement, he was looking at her and she knew he'd noticed something was up.

'Are you all right? You look as though you've seen a ghost.'

'I'm fine,' she said. 'Just a bit shocked.' She wanted to tell him who she'd just seen but couldn't find the words. How silly was that? It was probably nothing. On the other hand . . .

They began walking towards the park entrance.

'Nothing much shocks me, you know,' Geoff said. 'Some of the stuff people confide in me would make your hair curl, as my dear mum would say. Do you want to tell me about it?'

Geoff pointed to an empty bench beneath a tree.

'Shall we sit for a while? Then you can tell me what's bothering you, if it'll help.'

Fiona decided it might well help. It also occurred to her that, had it been Katie and Tim walking past, they could have wondered why Geoff and Fiona were spending time together after work. Well, Tim might, anyway. Katie knew her boss and Geoff were good friends as they'd been thrown together by circumstances.

'It's probably nothing,' Fiona began,

before updating him about Katie's anonymous visitor.

She described how taken aback she was to find her friend had left for the day without saying a word to her. She explained how this didn't fit their usual routine and Geoff nodded.

'While you and I were waiting to cross the road,' she said, 'I happened to glance through the café window. Seeing Katie and one of our male clients with their heads together gave me quite a start.

'Why would she agree to go out with a client, especially when her husband's due back from his cruise liner duties very soon?'

'There could be a perfectly simple explanation,' Geoff said.

But Fiona would have none of it.

'Katie gave me one very important rule — something that my great-aunt advised her about. Millie felt we should never, ever, become emotionally involved with a client. And those two back there looked pretty emotionally involved to me!' She blinked away tears.

Silently, Geoff handed her a snow-white handkerchief.

'You can let me have it back,' he said softly.

Katie wiped her eyes, hoping her mascara hadn't run. She blew her nose and sat staring into the distance. A wood pigeon was cooing somewhere overhead. The world hadn't come to an end, even if she felt like it had.

'Maybe your client suggested going to the café as the time was getting on?'

'We always offer to make a drink for clients and we quite often work on a bit later, just as you do. But I bet you don't take any of your female clients to the café!'

'No, I don't,' Geoff admitted, 'but from what I know of Katie, she's not a person who'd start seeing another man — especially not when we know she's longing to see her husband again. That doesn't make sense, Fiona.' He glanced sideways at her.

'Understandably you're annoyed that your co-worker appears to be taking matters in her own hands,' he went on, 'and choosing to leave the office with a client for whatever reason.

'You are the one Millie chose to continue her business so I suggest you have a quiet word with Katie tomorrow. Officially, she left the office at the close of her working day, so make it clear you're not complaining but tell her you saw her with this man and ask her what's going on.

'Otherwise, you'll fret and be suspicious and that will eventually damage your working relationship. But this is your decision.'

They sat in silence for a while and Fiona wondered why she still felt so miserable.

But Geoff hadn't finished yet.

'But I wonder what worries you most, Fiona? The fact that Katie's married and spending time with one of your male clients? Or the fact that it's this particular client?'

★ ★ ★

Tim had felt guilty about inviting Katie to accompany him to the café. Showered and changed into his civvies, he had charged up the stairs to find her, hoping he wouldn't run into Fiona, as his emotions were running high.

No sooner had Katie shut the door behind him than he began by updating her about his newfound friendship with Belinda.

'Something always seems to stop me from going any further than an initial meeting.'

'It was rough luck, getting stuck on that train,' she said, 'but we haven't given up on you, Captain Carlisle.'

He sank into the seat.

'It's Tim, remember? It's also confession time.'

Katie said nothing.

Something made him glance at his watch.

'Oh heck, I'm keeping you late. But I truly need to speak to you and not to Fiona.'

'I don't understand . . .'

'No, of course you don't. I wonder, in view of the time, could we continue this conversation elsewhere? Maybe that little café I passed on my way here? If possible, I'd prefer not to meet your boss, for reasons I'll explain if you allow me.'

She raised her eyebrows.

'All right. It's best you get downstairs right away, then. Fiona's in with a client and I'll follow you as soon as I lock my office and grab my handbag. I hope she won't think I'm rude, rushing off without telling her, but this is obviously serious stuff.'

* * *

They made their way to the café where Tim ordered their drinks at the counter while Katie found two seats where they'd have their backs to the other customers.

'This is very mysterious, Tim,' she said when he took his place beside her.

'I could say the same about Mrs Maple. Fiona isn't married, is she?' he asked. 'I got it wrong but why does she let people assume she is?'

Katie gave him a long, hard stare and he knew she'd picked up on what this was all about.

'No, she isn't married, but I assume all the clients who've registered since she took over believe that she is. Even though she doesn't wear a wedding ring.'

He leaned closer.

'But not only have I been unobservant, I also think I'm a colossal idiot. What do you think, Katie?'

She waited while two strawberry milk-shakes were placed before them, then leaned closer too.

'Are you trying to tell me what I think you're telling me, Tim?'

'I think you've guessed anyway.' He was staring at the crowd of pedestrians waiting to cross the road, but without taking any notice of them.

'You have feelings for Fiona.' A statement not a question.

'I have indeed.'

'So, what exactly has brought on this confession and what do you think I can do about it?'

Tim took a swallow of his drink.

'I need you to help me hatch a plot.'

★ ★ ★

Early next morning, Fiona arrived at her desk early. She still burned to ask Katie what was going on, but talking to Geoff had helped her enormously and had even given her a reasonable night's sleep.

She didn't want to quarrel with her co-worker who'd taught her so much about Millie's business and who Fiona thought of as a friend. But she dreaded confronting Katie, even though she felt there must be a logical explanation for what happened.

She heaved a huge sigh of relief when Katie arrived in the office bang on time and called out a greeting before putting her head round Fiona's door to tell her she had something significant to discuss.

Katie lost no time in reaching the point.

'I don't know if you realised it, but

Tim Carlisle called yesterday. He was worried about keeping me late, so he asked if I'd go to the café with him so he could speak to me in confidence.'

That hurt. Really hurt. But Fiona only nodded her head.

'Please, Fiona, don't look like that. He's embarrassed over the introductions that haven't worked out for him.'

'Is he giving up on us?' Fiona didn't know whether she felt relieved or devastated.

'Far from it! Although he's certain he and the Fragrant One are destined to be just buddies, he's come up with a scheme and wanted to sound me out first.'

Katie sat back in her chair.

'What kind of scheme?'

'He'd like you to be there when he has his next meeting with whoever we've chosen for him.'

'What! He can't be serious. How does he reckon that's even possible?'

'Just listen to me, please. He's suggested that after he makes a date with the next person, he'll tell us where and when, and he'll book a table for two, plus a table nearby for one.'

'That's a stupid idea! What would be the point?'

'Our handsome pilot says he's like a walrus at a tea party when he's trying to impress. He thinks he could do with some advice on how to charm a girl.'

'He should try to be natural, not try to impress. The man's impossible!'

'He thinks that if you can listen to him talking one to one, over dinner, you should be able to tell him where he's going wrong. He trusts you, Fiona. Believe me.'

Fiona could barely breathe. Slowly, oh so slowly, she'd come to realise how much the pilot appealed to her. That soft golden cowlick of hair that he shook out of the way now and then. His kindly brown eyes. They'd lit up the last couple of times she and Tim had met face to face.

How could she spy on him while he tried to charm another young woman? It would be sheer torture.

And yet, this was her business. Love and companionship in all its forms was its life blood. And if Tim Carlisle wanted her to eat dinner, while eavesdropping, then it was all in a good cause. Maybe it would put an end to her daydreaming.

She was miles away when Katie's voice interrupted her musings.

'Fiona? What do you think? I offered to go myself, but Tim wouldn't hear of it,' Katie said.

'I can't say I'm over the moon at the thought, but he obviously still hopes to meet the right girl, so I suppose I must do as he asks.' Now she knew what people meant when they talked about having a heavy heart.

'I did point out it wouldn't be ideal, dining on your own beside a couple, even though it was for work purposes, but Tim thought you and me might attract attention if we were eating together while appearing to be eavesdropping!'

'Good point. Don't worry about me, Katie. On my own I should be able to hear every word and I can take a book and pretend to read between courses.'

She tried to harden her heart.

'If Captain Carlisle wants to pay for three dinners, I'll do my best to give him his money's worth.' She paused.

'I'd like you to do all the arranging, Katie, if you don't mind. Best if you don't tell me who's turning up to meet Tim so I have no idea of her personality beforehand. What do you think?'

This Had Better be Good!

Tim received a phone call while wondering whether his freshly laundered uniform shirt really needed ironing. It was a female voice.

'Katie from Mrs Maple's office here, Tim. You'll be pleased to hear, all being well, Fiona has agreed to be at your chosen restaurant and will expect you to inform us of the details as soon as we've fixed your next introduction.'

He played along with her, not knowing whether Fiona was within earshot or not.

'That's very kind of her,' he said. 'I hope I don't let her down.'

He heard Katie almost splutter.

'It's OK, I waited for the boss to pop out to the shop before I rang. Unknowingly, Fiona played right into my hands and said it was best I arranged the appointment so she knew nothing about the young lady's background or character.

'I'd better make up a fake index card but I think I can get away with telling a few white lies about the person having only just registered and in my opinion being suitable for you.'

'Good grief, Katie, you'd make a good detective.'

'Or even criminal! Seriously, I may need to remind you of that when Fiona finds out what we've done. It's not the kind of thing I'd envisaged. I'm only agreeing to help because I think the pair of you won't get together otherwise.'

'I'm very grateful to you. I know what high principles your boss has. All I can hope is that she really does feel the same about me as I do about her.'

'Have faith! But I need to talk to a close friend and ask if she'll help us out. She's a member of her local amateur dramatic group and I think she'll enjoy this unusual role. I hope so anyway.'

'Yes, no way could we involve one of the registered clients in this — Fiona would hit the roof and quite rightly so.'

'I'm sure you'll be able to act in such a

way that no-one would blame my friend for making some excuse to abandon you after the main course.'

'Fiona thinks I must be trying too hard and still making a mess of things. Maybe I'll just be my usual boring self. This whole business is far more complicated than piloting a jumbo jet, I can tell you!'

Katie giggled.

'For you, it is! Tim, I'd better go now. I'll ring my friend from home this evening so you'd better give me a couple of dates when you're not flying.'

'Hang on.' He looked at his calendar. 'I'm not working or on standby on Monday or Tuesday.'

'Fine. My friend works near Leicester Square if that helps you choose a restaurant.'

'Good thinking. If she agrees, ask her if six-thirty would be convenient, would you?'

'I will. That time should suit Fiona, too. We mustn't forget her.'

Tim felt a thrill fizz down his spine.

'Affirmative, ma'am.'

Fiona refused to change from her office clothes.

'I'll go and freshen up but I need to merge into the background, don't I?'

'Um, I suppose so, but why don't you wear your pretty green dress? Go on, Fiona, you never know who you might meet!'

'Oh well, I suppose I ought to make the effort. What sort of food does the restaurant do?'

'Milligan's is a steak house. I did say.'

'It must've slipped my mind. I take it the young lady isn't vegetarian?'

'Correct.'

'Good.' Fiona checked her watch. 'I'll go upstairs then and leave you to lock up. Have a nice evening.'

'Thanks. I'll be thinking of you. Don't forget your book.'

★ ★ ★

Tim hoped he didn't mess this up. He'd been the one to come up with this crazy idea and now he must see it through. He caught a tube train that took him to Leicester Square far too early for his appointment, but he hadn't wanted to risk running into Fiona.

For two pins he'd turn right round and head off home because, although he was trained to react fast in an emergency, regarding matters of the heart, he was a mere learner. But how he longed for the opportunity to try!

He wandered around Leicester Square in the evening sunshine, reminding himself that this time he needed to sound boring rather than interesting. If he dazzled his guest, Fiona might decide he was doing fine and ruin his plan by leaving him to it!

Tim took the next turning and walked towards the restaurant where the receptionist greeted Tim and found his name on the bookings list.

'Ah.' The receptionist frowned. 'Captain Carlisle, table for two with a table for one nearby. Surely this should be a table for three, sir?'

Tim glanced round nervously. It was time for one of the white lies Katie had supplied.

'No, thanks. I'm an author and I'm working on a new novel. My companion and I will talk while the young lady seated nearby takes note of how much she can hear and whether my conversation sounds authentic.'

The waiter was listening, open-mouthed.

'Right, sir. As long as there's no trouble. We have our reputation to consider.' He peered at Tim. 'Haven't I seen you in here wearing airline uniform? With another pilot, if I remember rightly?'

'You have a good memory. Yes, you're quite correct. I work as a pilot but I'm trying to write a book in my off-duty time.' He'd need to mop his brow at this rate.

'I'll show you to your table, sir.'

Tim settled himself and requested a glass of water just as the door opened and Fiona came through it. He was facing the entrance and his insides turned to jelly as he saw the girl of his dreams. He took out his pocket diary and leafed through the pages, keeping his head down while a waiter escorted Fiona to her table.

She was seated a little way beyond his left shoulder and when he turned his head slightly, he could see her, looking fresh and lovely in a lime green dress.

The wine waiter was hovering and Tim heard Fiona order a glass of white wine. He saw her opening a menu. He wished Katie's friend would turn up so the play-acting could begin and for the umpteenth time, he hoped the charade wouldn't turn into a catastrophe.

Two couples came through the door, followed by three girls, dressed for a night out. There was a gentle buzz of conversation and laughter but not from Tim and Fiona's side of the restaurant. Where could this young woman have got to?

He felt contrite as he thought of the afternoon he had been held up and kept Jenny, who he never got to meet, as Fate had stepped in, waiting for far too long. Should he take matters into his own hands and confront Fiona with the truth?

The door opened to admit a young woman. But, as Tim glanced towards her, he saw the newcomer was Katie. He heard Fiona's exclamation and he turned towards her and met her gaze. What he saw in her eyes made him long to take her in his arms and confess his feelings. She must be wondering what on earth was going on.

Tim's heart seemed to plummet as he gloomily rated his chances with her as probably zero. Back at the desk, Katie politely hovered, then muttered an explanation to the waiter who greeted her.

'Oh dear, Tim,' Fiona said. 'Looks as though your date has stood you up. But why on earth is Katie here, I wonder?'

'I think we're about to find out,' he said as Katie threaded her way through the tables.

Tim got to his feet.

'Katie, let me order you a drink.'

'I won't say no,' she said. 'I'll have the same as Fiona if I may. It might help calm my nerves.'

Tim caught the waiter's eye and pulled out the vacant chair for Katie. He turned to Fiona.

'Why don't we all sit at the same table while Katie explains what's happened to my date? You can bawl me out afterwards.'

Fiona gazed at him in astonishment.

'I haven't the foggiest idea what you're talking about but do sit back down, Tim, and I'll move over.'

'First of all,' Katie began, 'I'm here because my friend decided she wanted to see me before coming to meet you, Tim. We hadn't seen each other for ages and it seemed only fair for me to meet her for a coffee and catch-up.'

Fiona looked from her friend to her client then back again. Tim could remember seeing a similar look on his instructor's face one unforgettable day when he'd succeeded in making a simulated landing like a toddler skidding on ice and landing on his backside, according to his much-respected mentor, Gus.

'Go on,' Fiona said.

'After I locked up the office, I set off to meet Lindsay at the tube station but just as I climbed the steps up to street level, I heard a voice calling me and saw her on the flight below.

'She'd spotted me, but she missed her footing and collapsed on the steps in a heap. People were helping her up but the worst thing was, she collided with someone hurrying down the steps. He was carrying a fizzy drink and he spilt it all over her pretty frock and just hurried off.

'Lindsay decided she couldn't bear to turn up for dinner, covered in orange juice, so I put her in a taxi home and came on here to give her apologies.'

'I'm the one who should be apologising,' Tim said. 'Maybe I'm right — I'm just bad news.'

Fiona had been looking from one to the other of them. Now she cleared her throat.

'I don't know what you two have been

playing at, but I fully intend finding out. Katie, will you stay and eat? I don't know about anyone else, but I'm ravenous and I get the feeling this could be a long night.'

Katie shook her head.

'I'm sorry, Fiona, but I need to get home before Mum and Dad send out a search party. In fact, I'll ask the man at the desk if I can make a phone call and tell them I'm on my way.'

'Why not ring them and say you're eating here first?'

Tim held his breath.

'Er, no, I'm afraid I'm too tired to stay, kind as it is of you to invite me. I'll see you in the morning, Fiona. I'm sure Tim will explain everything. You two should relax and enjoy your meal because, if you want my honest opinion, it's about time you sorted yourselves out!' She downed the rest of her wine and hurried off.

Fiona watched her go then looked at Tim.

'What is she talking about?' Fiona leaned across the table. 'Just tell me why

Katie set up a date between you and her friend. Because that's what she did, isn't it?'

'Only because I asked her!'

'But why involve me? By the sound of things, you and Katie were trying to mix agency business with a private introduction. Great-aunt Millie will be spinning in her grave!' She regarded him sternly.

'Please don't blame Katie for her part in this. I asked her to set up a fake date for me with one of her friends. She couldn't ask one of your clients, for obvious reasons.'

'Thank goodness for small mercies.' Fiona smiled up at the waiter as her gammon steak arrived.

'I came up with a plan and that plan backfired. Nothing malicious was intended and I'll explain every single detail to you so you know exactly what my intentions were.'

Fiona found it hard to believe she was actually eating dinner with the man she'd admired since she first set eyes upon

him. How many times had she fanta-
sised, conjuring up this very scene? But
she failed to see why he'd created such a
complicated situation.

'This had better be good,' she said.

'It's only fair to tell you everything, right
from the beginning, so you understand I
have no complaints whatsoever regarding
Mrs Maple's Marriage Bureau.'

'Well, that's a relief.' Fiona stabbed a
chip ferociously.

Tim winced.

'I understand how concerned you must
be and I know we've had our ups and
downs over the last couple of months.'

'The yellow socks.'

He saw her lips twitch.

'I thought you were being a little harsh
but I know you were trying to help me
succeed in finding a wife.'

She continued to attack her gammon
steak without meeting his gaze.

'That was the aim, yes.'

'It's been an interesting experience,
but it's made me realise something I
hadn't bargained for. So, I'm afraid I

must ask you to deregister me, if that's the correct term.'

That got her attention!

'Is that so? Then what possessed you to ask Katie, who I trust and rely on, to assist you in this bizarre plan? I really don't understand you, Tim.'

He put down his cutlery.

'Then it's a good job I understand myself, Fiona. Because for the first time in my life, I've fallen in love.'

It was as though what he said had come from somewhere far away. The man sitting opposite her had fallen in love. Fiona's brain must have gone on strike because she still didn't understand why she'd become involved in all this. And he was sitting there, gazing at her, with a very dreamy look upon his face. She'd never seen him look like that before.

'Congratulations,' she said. 'As long as the lucky lady feels the same?'

'I don't know yet,' he said. 'I haven't asked her.'

She still felt bemused.

'Is she one of our clients? Wait . . . no,

she can't be. If she is, you wouldn't have arranged this fiasco of an evening with someone else.'

'To be fair, I didn't know that poor girl was going to have an accident.'

'And if she hadn't? If she'd turned up, what was your plan?'

She watched him bite his lip.

'It was for me to be my usual clumsy self when trying to make a good impression. After Katie's friend had put up with me for as long as she could stand, she was to make an excuse and abandon me.'

'And after that?' Fiona hardly dared breathe.

'I would have asked if I could join you at your table. Then I was going to tell you what I've been longing to tell you for what feels like for ever.'

'You are the most maddening man I've ever met. Why can't you tell me now?'

'I'm about to. The girl I've fallen in love with is you, Fiona. No-one else but you.'

They sat on the train, rattling along beneath busy London's nightlife, each of them lost in thought. Fiona was regretting what she'd said to him and a swift glance sideways at Tim showed her how desolate he felt too.

She was still in shock but she'd been too angry with him to accept what he was saying. Why had he not approached her sooner, for goodness' sake? They left the train at Fiona's station and walked in silence to the escalator then through the barrier and to the exit.

'I can make my own way from here,' she said, trying to stifle a sob.

'All I can say is how sorry I am for being so stupid.'

She watched him turn from her and begin walking away. It was only as a double-decker trundled past that she saw sense and found her voice. He couldn't have heard her because he went on walking. Fiona began to run after him. Traffic stopped her from following.

Her fingernails bit into her palms. At last she made it across the road and yelled his name. He turned around and saw her.

Breathless, her cheeks wet with tears, she stood beneath a street lamp while he jogged back to her. As he stood in front of her and took her face between his hands, she managed to find the words.

'I love you, Timothy Carlisle. I've never felt like this before either.'

Not even a cheeky taxi-driver blasting his horn as he saw the kissing couple could stop either one of them from clinging on to the other as if they'd never let go again.

Other titles in the
Linford Romance Library:

A BODY IN THE CHAPEL

Philippa Carey

Ipswich, 1919: On her way to teach Sunday School, Margaret Preston finds a badly injured man unconscious at the chapel gate. She and her widowed father, Reverend Preston, take him in and call the doctor. When the stranger regains consciousness, he tells them he has lost his memory, not knowing who he is or how he came to be there. As he and Margaret grow closer, their fondness for one another increases. But she is already being courted by another man . . .

BLETCHLEY SECRETS

Dawn Knox

1940: A cold upbringing with parents who unfairly blame her for a family tragedy has robbed Jess of all self-worth and confidence. Escaping to join the WAAF, she's stationed at RAF Holsmere, until a seemingly unimportant competition leads to her recruitment into the secret world of code-breaking at Bletchley Park. Love, however, eludes her: the men she chooses are totally unsuitable — until she meets Daniel. But there is so much which separates them. Can they ever find happiness together?

THE LOMBARDI EMERALDS

Margaret Mounsdon

Who is Auguste Lombardi, and why has May's mother been invited to his eightieth birthday party? As her mother is halfway to Australia, and May is resting between acting roles, she attends in her place. To celebrate the occasion, she wears the earrings her mother gave her for her birthday — only to discover that they are not costume jewellery, but genuine emeralds, and part of the famous missing Lombardi collection . . .